Sun and fun . . .

Suddenly I saw the cutest guy!

He and some other guys were coming down to the beach behind us. Feeling kind of like a spy, I watched him. What a babe!

He was tall and had straight brown hair down to his shoulders. His eyes were bright blue. He was laughing at something one of his friends had said, and he had these superwhite teeth.

My heart started thumping like crazy.

That's when I realized that Mandy was talking to me.

"Jessica!" she was saying. "Hello? Are you there?" She leaned over Rachel and whispered, "I said that there are a lot of cute guys around."

"I noticed."

"Pippa said there's a club down by the pier. It's teens only tomorrow night. Let's go."

"Sounds like a plan," I said, already trying to decide which of my fabulous new sundresses to wear.

I looked back over my shoulder, wondering what the cute guy and his friends were doing. They were only a few yards away, and miracle of miracles, he looked right at me.

His blue eyes met mine, and he smiled.

Visit the Official Sweet Valley Web Site on the Internet at:

http://www.sweetvalley.com

SWEET VALLEY TWINS

Jessica: Next Stop, Jr. High

Written by
Jamie Suzanne

Created by
FRANCINE PASCAL

BANTAM BOOKS
NEW YORK • TORONTO • LONDON • SYDNEY • AUCKLAND

To Jenna Sanitsky

RL 4, 008-012

JESSICA: NEXT STOP, JR. HIGH
A Bantam Book / December 1998

Sweet Valley High® and Sweet Valley Twins® are
registered trademarks of Francine Pascal.

Conceived by Francine Pascal.

*Produced by 17th Street Productions,
a division of Daniel Weiss Associates, Inc.
33 West 17th Street
New York, NY 10011.*

Photography by Michael Segal.

ISBN: 0-553-48607-1

Published simultaneously in the United States and Canada

Bantam Books are published by Bantam Books, a division of Bantam
Doubleday Dell Publishing Group, Inc. Its trademark, consisting of the
words "Bantam Books" and the portrayal of a rooster, is Registered in the
U.S. Patent and Trademark Office and in other countries. Marca
Registrada. Bantam Books, 1540 Broadway, New York, New York 10036.

PRINTED IN THE UNITED STATES OF AMERICA

OPM   0 9 8 7 6 5 4 3 2 1

One

◇

Dear Jess,

Surprise!!!

By the time you read this, I'll be well on my way to Costa Rica. I ran back upstairs and put this on your pillow just before we all left to go to the airport this morning. I wanted to surprise you, but it's too bad I won't see your smile when you find this purple-fabric-covered notebook when you get home.

It's a diary.

I'm writing this note in the first few pages of *your* diary because I know how hard it is to face a blank page. I figured I'd sort of break it in for you. I guess you're wondering why I'm giving you a present when it's not your birthday. It's a "going-away present" even though *I'm* the one who's gone away.

Now don't start crying (again). I'm sure you've

already depleted your tear ducts on the ride home from the airport.

Was Steven nice, or did he torture you by telling you how many people die of snakebites in the rain forest? I'm guessing he opted for torture. I'm also guessing that Mom and Dad spent the entire ride home from the airport telling him to stop teasing you. But since they were trying (unsuccessfully) not to laugh, it just encouraged him. (Do I have ESP or what?)

Don't listen to anything he says. I'm going to be just fine. And I'm going to have a great time. Building houses in the Costa Rican rain forest is right up my alley.

Still, I'll miss you. Try not to forget what I look like. (Hee, hee!) Of course, if you do forget, you could just look in the mirror. See that girl with blue-green eyes, long blond hair, and the dimple? That's you.

I look exactly the same.

Seriously, Jess, the only thing that's worrying me about going to Costa Rica is leaving you here in Sweet Valley. I know that you and Lila haven't been so tight lately and your summer's not working out the way you had hoped. I've been getting the feeling you're a little lonely. (See! I *do* have ESP.)

All I know is that when *I'm* feeling lonely, writing in my diary helps. So if you start to feel lonely or worried—remember the Elizabeth Wakefield motto: Scribble! It works.

I'll see you in a month, and I'll think about you every single day.

Love,
Elizabeth

P.S. Please try not to murder Steven while I'm gone.
P.P.S. Or Lila Fowler.

SUNDAY, 6:30 P.M..

Dear Diary,

I don't know if having an identical twin with ESP is good or bad. I *did* cry all the way home from the airport. Steven *did* tell me that the snakes in Costa Rica were a thousand feet long and could swallow an average-sized thirteen-year-old girl whole. Mom and Dad *did* tell him to keep quiet. They *did* laugh hysterically when he did his imitation of Elizabeth being swallowed by a giant snake. And yes, I *did* want to murder him.

"No, no," Steven screamed in this really high voice that was supposed to be Elizabeth's. "I haven't finished my homewooooooooork!" He trailed off and finished with a great big gulp and belch that was supposed to be the snake.

Even I had to laugh at that last part. Does that make me a horrible person?

I guess not. In fact, I know I'm a wonderful person. Because I love Elizabeth even though she is a straight-A student, five thousand times more responsible than I am, and always doing something to help other people or save the world. Only a very mature and incredibly fabulous sister could love a sister like *that*. (Ha-ha!)

I'm glad I had a little surprise present of my own for Elizabeth, which I gave her at the airport. It was a bag of CDs and movie magazines. I know Elizabeth is looking forward to going deep into the rain forest and leaving civilization behind. But who could spend a whole month with no rock and roll and no celebrity gossip?

Anyway, when I got home and found this diary, I thought it was a nice idea—a very Elizabeth idea. But I really couldn't see myself writing in it.

Elizabeth's been gone for twelve hours, though, and I've just got to talk to someone. These days there's no point at all in trying to talk to my so-called best friend, Lila Fowler.

If I talk to Lila, I'll have to hear all about what Wiley said. And what Wiley did. And what Wiley thinks. Blah, blah, blah. Wiley, Wiley, Wiley. Brag, brag, brag.

If I hear one more word about Wiley Upjohn, I'm going to *upchuck.*

I can't believe how Lila is letting this I-have-a-boyfriend-and-you-don't thing go to her head. It's not even like he's that cute. He's definitely not that tall. Maybe half an inch taller than Lila. *Maybe!*

The only thing Wiley Upjohn has going for him is the fact that he's in high school—or he will be in September. This is something that Lila manages to work into our conversations about every two seconds.

Wiley Upjohn is ruining my whole summer.

And it was supposed to be the best summer of my life. The summer I would always remember. The summer before eighth grade.

The last summer of the Unicorns.

See, this might be the Unicorns' last summer together as a club. It's hard to believe, but I might not be going to Sweet Valley Middle School next year. Our school district has been rezoned. Nobody knows yet which school they will be going to in September.

Before we heard about the rezoning plan, all the Unicorns were psyched about going into the eighth grade. Being in eighth grade isn't like being in high school, but it's still a pretty big deal because you're finally at the top of the middle-school heap.

And let me tell you, I'd waited a long time for this.

When I joined the Unicorn Club two years ago, I was a sixth-grader. Janet Howell (she was president of the club then) was an eighth-grader. During that first year Janet and the seventh-graders really made me and the other sixth-graders jump through hoops. And boy, did we jump!

Why? Because the Unicorn Club was made up of the prettiest and most popular girls at Sweet Valley Middle School. Everyone wanted to be a Unicorn, and I was no different. I mean, no matter how bossy Janet Howell got and no matter how mean the other Unicorns acted, I hung in there because I wanted to be part of the club.

Then last year Janet Howell went on to high school (thank goodness—I mean, she was my friend and all, but let's face it—the girl could be a total nightmare sometimes) and some other members dropped out. The only people left were me, Ellen Riteman, Lila Fowler, Mandy Miller, Rachel Grant, and Kimberly Haver.

We elected Ellen Riteman president. Ellen was a way cooler leader than Janet. Ellen's nice even if she is a little ditzy. OK, make that a *lot* ditzy. But she did a good job of holding the club together and didn't let the power go to her head.

So all in all, everybody was happy last year. And everybody was the same age. Everybody except Kimberly, that is.

She's a year older than the rest of us, so she was an eighth-grader while we were seventh-graders. Even though she wasn't the president, Kimberly couldn't resist pulling rank on us now and then.

Don't get me wrong. I love Kimberly. She's one of my best friends, and I'm going to miss her next year when she's at high school. But before I heard about the rezoning thing, I had decided that I wasn't completely heartbroken that she was leaving Sweet Valley Middle School. Because once Kimberly was gone, that meant that all the remaining Unicorns would be eighth-graders. We'd all be equals. Nobody could make me do things I didn't want to do anymore.

But now if we split up and go to different schools, there won't even *be* a Unicorn Club next year. That's why this is the last summer of the Unicorns.

We all made a solemn vow to make the most of

it and to spend as much time together as we could. I was psyched to have the best summer ever.

I was, like, *so* naive.

Everything started off great. But somewhere in the first week of July, Lila showed up at Casey's Ice Cream Parlor with Wiley Upjohn. That's when everything changed.

Janet Howell, our former president who is now a sophomore in high school, is Lila Fowler's cousin. Turns out it was Janet who set Lila up with Wiley.

Janet said that since Wiley was going to be in the ninth grade and Lila was going to be in the eighth grade, it was a perfect match. Lila would get to go to all the high-school dances, etc. *Plus*—she would have a cool date for all the eighth-grade parties no matter which school she ended up at.

That was the end of the "equality" dream. Let's face it, having a boyfriend gives you a lot of clout in a club like ours. Getting a high-school boyfriend was like taking a quantum prestige leap.

Within a week of dating Wiley, Lila was "unavailable to hang." Whenever I called her, she was on her way to meet Wiley somewhere.

When she *is* available to do stuff—with me and the rest of the Unicorns—she acts like a Janet Howell clone. Laying down "the rules according to Lila." Telling us how to act if we want high-school guys to like us. Telling us how to dress. Who the cool bands are and what songs we should memorize. Stuff like that.

Now everybody's worrying about what Lila thinks and whether they're acting cool enough.

And Lila's version of acting cool can be a drag.
None of the Unicorns acts interested or excited
about anything or anybody anymore.

I wish Lila and Wiley had never gotten together.
It's ruining everything.

SUNDAY, 8:00 P.M.

Dear Diary,
I'm back. Lila just called me, and guess who she
yakked, yakked, yakked my ear off about?

Wiley, of course.

It sounds horrible, but I almost hope Lila and I
do wind up going to different schools next year. I
just don't think I can stand having to hang out with
Lila and listen to her gloat.

MONDAY, 12:00 P.M.

Dear Diary,
I just read over what I wrote yesterday. I realized
that I sounded totally jealous. Gee, what a surprise.
Because I *am* totally jealous.

This last week has been a major bummer.
Kimberly and her folks are at Waterworks, this fabulous new theme park. Mandy's grandmother is
here, so she doesn't have time to do anything.
Rachel and her dad went to his company golf tournament in Arizona. And Ellen's dad took her and
her little brother on a camping trip.

I'm totally bored. I've got nobody to hang with—
I've been forced to do stuff *all by myself!* And every
single time I leave the house, I wind up running

into Lila and Wiley. I went to the mall and there they were. I went to a movie, and they sat down *right behind me*. I took a walk, and they were sitting on a park bench holding hands. I pretended not to see them and got out of there *fast*.

According to Lila, Wiley's going on some boat trip with his family next week and she just doesn't know how she's going to "survive the separation." (I wanted to—but did not—puke when she told me that.)

Maybe it's a good thing everybody has been out of town. If anybody had been around to listen, I probably would have said something really nasty about Lila and I would have looked as jealous as I feel.

Only you know how rotten I feel, Diary.

I probably couldn't even talk to Elizabeth about this. She thinks the Unicorns are, like, the most superficial bunch of airheads in Sweet Valley. She would think I was totally dumb for letting myself get all upset.

She would also tell me that I should have planned something for myself this summer besides hanging with the Unicorns because they're not the kind of girls you can count on.

But I didn't *want* to do anything else this summer. I wanted to spend time with my friends. I wanted it to be like old times. I especially wanted to spend time with Lila. My "best friend." How could I know she would hook up with Wiley Upjohn and have no time for me?

It probably wouldn't bother me so much if it were any other Unicorn. But Lila and I have been competing our whole lives, and Lila always wins. Always. It's so *frustrating*.

Lila Fowler's dad is Mr. Fowler. That's Fowler as in Fowler Enterprises.

Mr. Fowler is a multigabillionaire, and Lila is an only child. Her folks are divorced, and her mom lives in Europe somewhere. The "no mom" deal makes Lila's dad feel so guilty, he spoils Lila to death.

Get this—*Lila has her own car!!!*

She can't even drive—*but she has a car!!!* The chauffeur drives her around in it. She has her own charge cards. She has *everything.*

It's not fair.

And now she's got a boyfriend in high school and *I hate her guts!*

I don't think I'm going to write in this diary anymore. It's not making me feel better. It's making me feel worse.

I'm outta here, and there goes the phone.

MONDAY, 12:35 P.M.

Dear Diary,

Good news! I can stop feeling sorry for myself now.

When the phone rang, it was Rachel.

Rachel Grant is as rich as Lila is. She and her dad live in a big mansion right next door to the Fowlers.

Anyway, Rachel and her dad are back from the golf tournament, and she's having a slumber party tonight. Everybody is coming back today, so the whole club will be there—even Lila.

It's about time!

I don't know if I'm the only one who's feeling sentimental about this last-summer-of-the-Unicorns thing, but somehow it's just really important to me that we all spend some time together. Honestly, I'm a little scared about next year. What if I'm the only one who has to go to a new school? What if nobody likes me there?

Oh, ugh. I can't start thinking about that now—I need to start figuring out what to wear to the slumber party!

Two

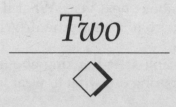

Dear Diary,
   Things change!!!
   Big news!!!
   Great news!!!
   I'm not a writer, so it's hard to know where to start. So much stuff has happened since I last wrote anything.
   I guess I'll start at the beginning of Rachel's slumber party.
   When I got to Rachel's, Ellen and Mandy were already in the living room, listening to the latest addition to Rachel's incredible CD collection. Mandy was dancing. Her eyes were closed, and she bounced her head back and forth, letting her hair flop. When she opened her eyes and saw me, she broke into a big sunny smile and blew me a kiss.

Mandy's one Unicorn who'll never be "too cool to care." She's a very friendly, sweet, sincere person. These days she's majorly emotional too. She'll cry over anything. Everything is, like, a "major moment."

Mandy started wearing beaded braids over the summer. She's also got some green and pink extensions. It's a great look for her. Very Mandy. Only hipper. Mandy's always had a lot of fashion flair. She's got long thick brown hair, big green eyes, and a powerful imagination. She could probably walk into a hardware store and come out with a great outfit.

Ellen has done some major appearance improving too. She still has her straight brunette bob, but she's cut her bangs supershort. She was wearing really good makeup and way wide jeans with a ribbed top. Ellen's tall and kind of lanky, so it was a good look on her. She twirled across the living room like a model and gave me a hug—which made me feel good. "What do you think? There was an outlet mall in the town near the campgrounds. Dad sprang for a shopping spree. I wish you had been with me, though. It just doesn't feel like a shopping spree without you."

"I think you look great," I told her.

All my worries were slipping away. Nobody was acting *hipper than thou.*

Rachel hugged me too and then plopped a cap on my head. The Grant Open was printed across the top. "A present from the tournament," she told me. "I brought one for everybody. I really missed you guys."

Rachel looked great. Her dark brown skin was practically glowing. The only makeup she was wearing was red-tinted lip gloss. And she wore her hair in lots of dreads that hung almost to her shoulders.

I was really starting to feel better about everything. We were all together again. Tight. Friends.

"I love your outfit," Rachel told me.

"Really?" I hadn't felt completely sure about my tie-dyed slip dress and platform mules. It was a little over the top for me. During one of my long and lonely afternoons I went to the mall and drowned my sorrows in a cheeseburger and sale shopping.

"It's great," Rachel said. "You look like a highschooler. *Hey!* Turn down the music," Rachel yelled at Mandy. "I think the pizza guy is here."

Mandy turned off the music, and Rachel ran into the front hall. She threw open the door and let out this loud guffaw.

Mandy and Ellen came into the front hall to see what Rachel was laughing about. I went too. When I saw, I started to laugh so hard, I almost fell off my platforms.

It wasn't the pizza guy. It was Kimberly.

I swear she looked two inches taller than she was the last time I saw her. They must put something in the water at Waterworks. Miracle-Tall or something.

Kimberly is very athletic—and she had obviously spent a lot of time swimming. Her light sunburn made her blue eyes look even bluer. And her pink face went well with her exotic getup.

She had on an extra-large Hawaiian shirt, long baggies, and some dopey grass skirt over them.

Kimberly started swaying back and forth while singing a song that was probably supposed to sound like a Hawaiian guitar but came out sounding like a cat with a really bad cold.

"This isn't a theme party," Rachel told her. "But I like your costume anyway."

Kimberly grinned, reached into her tote, and produced a necklace of flowers. She placed it over Rachel's neck. "Yes, it's true," she said in a game-show-announcer voice. "You, Rachel Grant, and all of the Unicorns have won a fabulous, all-expenses-paid trip to Hawaii!"

"What?" we asked, and everybody sort of stared at everybody else.

Kimberly grinned, whipped off the grass skirt, and pulled a letter out of her bag. "You guys have heard me talk about Aunt Pippa, right?"

"Yes," Ellen said.

"No," Rachel said.

"I can't remember," I said.

Kimberly pushed her wavy dark hair back off her face.

"Aunt Pippa is my dad's sister. She's never gotten married, and she was a surf bum for years. Actually she wasn't a surf *bum*, she was a surfing *champion*. But it drove my dad crazy anyway. He thinks everybody should get a job and live like he does. Anyway, two years ago she won the lottery."

"That is so cool!" Ellen said, and gave a low whistle.

"It was," Kimberly agreed. "Because she bought this chain of surfing shops in Hawaii and got really successful, and now she lives in this big luxury condo on the island of Oahu. Anyway, her present to me for graduating eighth grade is a house party. She's going to treat me to tickets for the whole club to fly out to Hawaii and spend the month of August at her condo. Basically the rest of the summer. She even bought the tickets already!"

There was this stunned silence. Like nobody could believe it. Then we just went nuts.

Ellen screamed like a game-show contestant. I jumped up and down until I realized that I could break my neck in those platforms I was wearing. Rachel hooked her arm through Kimberly's, and they started twirling each other around. And Mandy just started to cry.

That's when Lila walked in.

We all tried to tell her what was going on, but we weren't making any sense, so we quieted down and Kimberly delivered the thrilling news all over again complete with hula dance.

And did Lila have the common courtesy to look thrilled? Scream? Jump up and down?

No.

First thing out of her mouth: "I've been to Hawaii so many times, I'm not sure I really want to go again. Besides, I don't want to be away from Wiley that long."

I felt like somebody had just kicked me in the stomach. Hurt, yeah. But also too surprised to react.

"But he left *you* to go out of town," Rachel pointed out. (Two points, Rachel.)

Lila looked irritated that anybody mentioned it. Then she glanced at her watch. "Oh! He should be calling me about now." She gave Rachel and me this sickening smile. "He calls every day that we're apart."

"He only left this morning," I pointed out.

Of course, Lila didn't appreciate that remark, but I didn't say anything else because really and truly, I didn't want to make her so mad that she wouldn't come to Hawaii.

She might be making me sick to my stomach these days, but she's still my best friend. It just wouldn't feel like a Unicorn trip without her.

Sure enough, the little mobile phone in her purse started to ring, and Lila answered it in this silly, breathy falsetto. "Hello-o-o-o?"

It was Wiley. She took the phone into the living room and stayed in there for about an hour.

The rest of us wandered into the den off the living room so that Lila could have some privacy. Everybody was totally excited about going to Hawaii. We couldn't stop talking and giggling. Mandy was boo-hoo-hooing because she was "so touched" that Kimberly's aunt was giving her such a great present. And she was "so touched" that Kimberly had thought about all her friends. And she was "so touched" that Rachel was having this slumber party. And—

"Knock it off!" Kimberly begged. "If you don't stop, we'll all start bawling."

Everybody laughed at that—especially Mandy. Even *she* sees the humor in the fact that she's turned into the sentiment queen of Sweet Valley.

Then again, look who's talking. I've been feeling very sentimental myself. In fact, I was feeling so sentimental that I knew that the trip just wouldn't be fun for me at all if Lila didn't go.

Besides, I had a feeling that once we got to Hawaii, things would be different. Without Wiley around she'd be the old Lila again. A snot, sure. But a snot who had time for me and the rest of the club.

Finally Lila appeared in the doorway. My heart started pounding. I held my breath. *Please say you're going!* I thought. *Please! Please! Please!*

She took a ten-second dramatic pause before she announced—"Wiley says he wouldn't want me to give up a trip with my friends. He's very unselfish," she added. "So I'm going."

Then the old Lila came out. She grabbed my hands, and we started jumping up and down together. "Look out, Hawaii—here come the Unicorns!"

So now there's only one teeny-weeny hurdle left. The old parental permission slip.

TUESDAY, 5:00 P.M.

Dear Diary,

Here's how it went down.

I laid it out for Mom and Dad. I told them that Kimberly's aunt was treating us all to plane tickets and a month at her condo in Hawaii. I told them that the entire Unicorn Club was invited. And I told them that if they didn't let me go, it would ruin my whole life, destroy my emotional health, and make it impossible for me to ever finish my education and get a job. Dad said he was willing to take that chance.

I pointed out that not finishing school and getting a job would mean that I would have to live with *them* for the rest of my life.

Mom turned pale and called Kimberly's mom from our phone in the kitchen.

I went into the living room, grabbed the cordless, and hid in the hall closet so I could listen in on their conversation.

Kimberly's mom told Mom that the offer was for real. But Mrs. Haver also said that Pippa was "unconventional."

"Nuts!" I could hear Kimberly's dad yelling in the background. "She's not *unconventional*. She's *nuts!*"

Of course, that just made me more determined to go. But Mom got all concerned and told Mrs. Haver that she and my dad would have to talk it over.

I was less than thrilled. *We'll have to talk it over* is right up there with *We'll see.*

It means *no*.

I immediately called Kimberly on her line—the one that rings in her room. I told her that my parents were grumbling and that she should do something quick! Like put a gag on her dad and get her mother to call again.

A few minutes later the phone rang.

I listened in again. It was Mrs. Haver. She seemed pretty amused and told my folks that they shouldn't pay too much attention to anything Mr. Haver said because he was totally traditional and had a hard time relating to Pippa's lifestyle—which was more "relaxed" than most people's.

"Nuts!" I could hear him yelling. "Her approach to life is nuts!" (I guess Kimberly didn't get any co-operation with the gag request.)

Kimberly's mom shushed Mr. Haver, and then she told my folks that she had complete confidence in Pippa's ability to supervise and chaperon us during the trip.

"Then you're nuts too!" I heard Mr. Haver yell in the background. "She'll have them on the first plane back to Sweet Valley. Trust me."

Fortunately my parents think that Mrs. Haver is a very smart lady—and that Mr. Haver is wound a little too tightly.

So after making me sweat it out for a couple of hours while they "talked it over," Mom and Dad gave the project two thumbs-up. (Or would that be *four* thumbs-up?)

Oh—who cares? All that matters is that the answer is *"yes!"*

TUESDAY, 8 P.M.

Dear Diary,

Here's the update on permissions secured regarding Operation Hawaii:

Jessica—Go

Rachel—Go
Lila—Go
Mandy—Go
Ellen—Go
It's a go, Houston.
Ready for liftoff!

Three

◇

Dear Diary,

We've been on the plane now for about four hours. Lila started out sitting next to me, and we got along great for about the first thirty minutes. Then she zapped me.

"Jessica," she said. "I don't want to hurt your feelings. But there's something I've been wanting to tell you."

"What?" I asked. She sounded so serious, I thought she was going to tell me I smelled bad or something.

"It's about that tie-dyed dress."

"What about it?"

"Lose it," she said.

I stopped worrying about how I smelled. Suddenly a big wad of irritation balled up in my chest. "Why?" I asked, trying not to sound as peeved as I felt.

"Wiley and I saw you in Music Mania in that outfit, and he didn't like it."

I opened my magazine and stared at it hard. "Tough," I said, not looking at Lila.

"Don't get mad. I'm telling you this for your own good. Wiley says clothes like that make girls look like they're trying too hard to be noticed."

(I couldn't believe this was coming from somebody who rides around town in a chauffeur-driven car with vanity plates that say Lila Rules.)

But I didn't make any sarcastic remarks about the car since I enjoy riding around in it myself. So I just said, "Oh, yeah? Since when is Wiley Upjohn a girls' fashion expert?"

She groaned. "I knew you were going to be this way."

"What way?" I demanded.

"You're going to make things so hard on yourself." Lila sighed as if she felt sorry for me. "Next year is going to be a key year."

"What are you talking about?"

"Jessica! It's the year before we go to high school. Whatever rep we get in the eighth grade is going to follow us. You've got to get your image right this year. The last two years were all about experimenting. Now it's time to get serious."

As much as I wanted to tell her to go jump off the wing, I couldn't help thinking she might have a point. I'd been looking forward to eighth grade because I thought we could finally be who we wanted. Wear what we wanted. Hang out with who we wanted.

But the way Lila was putting it, it was going to

be worse than when we were sixth-graders. Because
if you make mistakes in the sixth grade, nobody
holds it against you. You're a sixth-grader; what do
you know? But it sounded like eighth-grade mistakes wound up on your permanent record.

On top of everything else—I might be, like, *a
new kid!*

"Just think about it," Lila urged, patting me on
the arm. Then she got up and went over to sit with
Kimberly for a while.

I looked out the window at the clouds. They
looked like cotton candy.

In spite of feeling irritated with Lila and worried
that I might ruin my whole life by wearing a tie-
dyed dress that Wiley Upjohn didn't like, my heart
just kind of soared. How could I be unhappy miles
up in the sky on my way to Hawaii?

Lila's just going through a phase. She's dating a
guy in high school, so she thinks she knows everything. She'll get over it once we get to Hawaii and
start having fun. (Or once Wiley dumps her for
some girl in high school.)

Once we get to Hawaii, it's going to be just like
the old days. All for one and one for all.

> WEDNESDAY, 8:30 P.M.
> (HAWAIIAN TIME—IT'S 10:30 IN SWEET VALLEY!)

Dear Diary,

Things change. I know I said that already, but I just
can't get over how *fast* things change. One minute
you're soaring through the clouds, and the next

minute you're hitting the ground with a hard thump.

I guess that was a metaphor. (Unless it's a simile. I'll have to look it up.) Whatever it is, it's pretty good. Maybe I can use it in a book report sometime. But I'm not going to think about book reports now. I've got enough to worry about.

Anyway, there I was flying through cotton candy, thinking everything was just great—and it *was* for a while.

The view as we were coming in for the landing was incredible. Hawaii is made up of lots of islands. There are eight main ones: Hawaii, Maui, Kahoolawe, Molokai, Lanai, Oahu, Kauai, and Niihau. From the air the islands looked like green jewels sprinkled across blue velvet.

We landed in Honolulu on the island of Oahu. We got our bags and felt really grown-up because we were going to get ourselves to the condo. Nobody met us or anything. Pippa had sent Kimberly a letter with instructions on how to get ground transportation.

Mandy read to us from Pippa's letter. Kimberly found the bus stop at the airport. Ellen figured out which bus was ours. Rachel bought the tickets. I made sure everybody's bags were stowed. And Lila got the driver to take a picture of us all standing in front of the bus.

We were a real team.

Pippa lives outside the city on the coast. As I looked out the window at the surf I didn't think it was possible to be any happier. I always thought California was beautiful, but Hawaii is like paradise.

Everywhere I looked, I saw trees, color, and ocean. It's gorgeous. It even smells good. Like tropical flowers, fruit salad, and salt water.

"This is going to be the best vacation ever," I said happily. "Sun, sand, and nothing but Unicorns."

Mandy pushed her extensions back off her shoulders and adjusted her Grant Open billed cap. "We're going to have such a good time. No parents."

"No obnoxious brothers and sisters!" Ellen added.

"No obnoxious sixth- and seventh-graders!" Rachel said with a laugh. "We'd better enjoy it now. Because in September we're going to be surrounded by them."

Everybody laughed. But I noticed that Kimberly turned red and looked out the window. I figured she was embarrassed. We tend to forget she's a year older. Maybe she thought we were making fun of her because *she* had been hanging with seventh-graders when she was an eighth-grader.

Before I could say anything, we hit a part of the beach that had tall buildings along it. Very fancy-looking buildings. Kimberly stood up. "This is our stop," she announced.

I noticed her voice sounded kind of flat. I hoped we hadn't hurt her feelings.

We all shouldered our bags, got off the bus, and crossed the street. It felt really strange to get off a bus and walk up to a luxury building on the beach. The doorman wore white pants and a Hawaiian shirt.

It was obvious he was expecting us because as soon

as he saw us he grinned and went inside for a big dolly. "Aloha!" he said as we piled our bags on top of it.

"*Aloha?*" Ellen giggled. "I thought that meant good-bye. We just got here."

"*Aloha* means hello *and* good-bye," he told us with a grin. "Welcome to Hawaii. I'm Mickey. Ms. Haver said I should take you right up."

We walked into the lobby of this gorgeous building and almost fell over, we were so dazzled. The building had a big atrium in the middle with a huge fish tank. The fish in it were so exotic, they didn't even look real.

Then we all got in this big glass elevator and went up, up, up. It was *très* plush. Even Lila and Rachel looked impressed.

Finally we were at the top.

"She has the penthouse?" Ellen asked Kimberly in a whisper.

Kimberly nodded. "I guess. I've never been here before. The last time I visited Pippa, she lived in a little one-room bungalow."

The elevator doors opened. There was only one apartment-door entrance on the whole floor. It was right across from the elevator. As soon as the elevator went *ding* the door to the apartment swung open.

"Hi!" This really young-looking person with braces opened her arms and threw them around Kimberly. "I'm so glad you guys are here. I've been waiting and waiting!"

"Wow," Ellen whispered to me. "Pippa looks even younger than us."

I rolled my eyes. Honestly, sometimes Ellen is so dense, it's hard to believe she finds her way to school. "That's not Pippa," I whispered back.

"Who is it?" Rachel asked.

I shrugged. I had no idea. But whoever it was had reddish brown shoulder-length curly hair, a sprinkle of brown freckles, and bright green eyes with thick lashes. She wore cutoffs and a big T-shirt that said Pippa Surf Shack.

Mickey rolled the bags into the living room, and Kimberly turned to us. "Guys, this is my cousin Marissa." She didn't look anybody in the eye when she said it. "Marissa, this is Jessica, Lila, Rachel, Mandy, and Ellen."

Marissa flashed us this big metallic grin. "Hi. We're going to have so much fun!"

"I thought Pippa didn't have any kids," Lila said. (Not bothering to whisper, of course.)

Marissa giggled. "I'm not Pippa's daughter. My mom is Renatta. She's Pippa's and Kimberly's dad's sister. Get it?" Then without waiting for an answer, she just kept on talking. "I've been here about two weeks already. It's been a blast. Pippa and I get along great. I've helped her do a lot of inventory and stuff at a couple of her stores. She's really busy these days. But now that you guys are here, we are going to party, party, *party!*"

She pretended to do the twist and then threw back her head, laughing like a donkey. Hee-haw!

Rachel was looking at her as if she were a talking monkey or something, but Marissa didn't notice.

She skipped—*(skipped)*—around the sofa and examined the big dolly piled with bags. "I was so glad to find out that most of you are eighth-graders. I was afraid that you guys wouldn't want to hang with me because I'm a seventh-grader," she babbled. "But if Kimberly hung with you when you were in seventh grade, then you guys obviously don't worry too much about the age thing."

She pointed at Rachel and Lila. (Rude!) "Mickey," she says, like she owns the place, "put these two in the room at the end of the hall."

Rachel's eyebrows rose until they practically disappeared into her hairline.

Lila's mouth dropped open—like she couldn't believe this little kid actually had the nerve to refer to her and Rachel as *these two.*

Then she pointed at me. "You and Kimberly can be in with me," Marissa continued. She looked at Ellen and Mandy and put a finger to her chin as if she were thinking. "I guess you two can sleep on the couches and use the bathroom in the hall. Just try to keep your stuff neat so the living room doesn't look like a mess, OK?"

Ellen shrugged, like she didn't care where she slept, but she looked sullen. I didn't blame her. Who would want to be told not to make a mess by a seventh-grader? It was insulting.

I shot a look at Kimberly. She was looking around the apartment, checking out the living room and the big attached kitchen. I waited for her to say or do something. But she didn't. Her face was red, and she wouldn't meet anybody's eyes.

I realized suddenly that Kimberly had known all along that Marissa was going to be here but hadn't told us. That's why she had looked so funny on the bus when Rachel made that comment about not having any seventh-graders around.

Rachel and Lila followed Mickey down the hall after flashing Kimberly a superdirty look.

"Come see our room," Marissa said eagerly. She grabbed Kimberly and me and started shoving us down the hall.

The room was really nice. Big. Two single beds and a roll-away cot over by the window. Marissa pointed to me. "You can have the cot." Then she pointed to one of the beds. "Kimberly, you can sleep here."

"When is Pippa coming back?" Kimberly asked.

Her voice was flat. Not unfriendly. But not warm and cousinly either.

"She'll be home soon," Marissa promised—completely oblivious to the fact that Kimberly seemed less than thrilled to see her. "But she left me money, and I'm supposed to go pick up dinner at the restaurant next door. I'm going now. Want to come with me? The headwaiter there is really nice. Cute, too. I think he likes me. He's probably about eighteen. His name is Luke, and he's from Idaho. He says his father came for a vacation and decided to stay for the rest of his life, so the whole family just up and moved. He has brown hair in a ponytail. Usually I like guys with blond hair, but—"

Yak, yak, yak. Was she ever going to shut up?

"I'll go see how Rachel and Lila are doing," I said, escaping out the door and leaving Kimberly with Marissa, the Amazing Babbler.

The bedroom door at the end of the hall was open, and I saw Rachel and Lila in there. Ellen too. I hurried in, and Ellen shut the door behind me.

"*Who* was that?" Rachel exclaimed.

"Kimberly's first cousin," Ellen answered, blinking. "Didn't you hear? Her mom is—"

"I know that, Ellen," Rachel snapped. "Get a clue or get out, would you?"

Ellen closed her mouth and looked hurt.

"Hey," I said softly. "Chill out." *We just got here and we're already arguing?* I thought. Not a good sign.

Rachel sighed. "I'm sorry, Ellen. It's just that this Marissa person came as kind of a shock. She could ruin our whole vacation. Talk about pushy!"

"That's OK," Ellen mumbled.

There was a soft knock at the door.

Lila popped up and opened it a crack. It was Kimberly.

Lila took her by the hand, pulled her into the room, and shut the door firmly. "*What* is that girl's problem?"

Kimberly rolled her eyes. "I know Marissa is hard to take. What can I say? She's always been that way."

"Did you know she was going to be here?" Rachel asked in her Rachel-for-the-prosecution voice.

Kimberly plopped down on the bed and sighed glumly. "Pippa told me she was visiting and might stay over until the end of the summer. But I didn't know for sure until this afternoon. Marissa's mom wasn't sure she wanted her to stay while we were here because we're older and everything. Marissa's very impressionable."

Lila sucked in her breath and got this real offended look on her face. "So Marissa's mom thinks we might be a bad influence on her little daughter?"

Kimberly shrugged. "Well . . . yeah."

There was a long silence while everybody tried to decide whether they felt insulted or flattered.

"She can't stay," Lila announced.

"You're going to have to do something," Rachel put in.

Kimberly pushed back her hair. "I'll talk to Pippa," she promised. "Maybe she can come up with some tactful way to send Marissa home."

There was another knock at the door.

Everybody froze. Was it Marissa?

Rachel got up and answered the knock with her face all twisted up in a big scowl. "Yes?" she growled, jerking open the door.

It was Mandy.

"Pippa's home," she said. "Come out into the living room and say hi."

It's hard to describe Pippa. I've never really known a grown person like her. She looks about my mom's age or maybe a little younger. But she has long blond hair to her waist and a deep tan, and she seems really cool.

When Pippa saw Kimberly, she grabbed her in a

hug, picked her up, and twirled her around. "You're so tall," she cried. "And I'm so glad to see you!"

Kimberly grinned. "Thanks for letting us come."

Pippa let go of Kimberly, draped her arm over her shoulders, and turned toward us. "Let me see if I can guess who these people are," she said. "My hobby is telepathy." She put her hand over her forehead and made this humming sound. Then she came over to where we stood.

"You're Jessica," she said, putting her hand on my head.

Then one by one she identified every single person. "Ellen, Rachel, Mandy, and Lila."

"That's amazing!" Rachel gasped. "How did you do that?"

Pippa let out this deep laugh, opened a drawer, and pulled out a photo. "From this."

We all gathered around and started to laugh. It was a picture of us taken last year. Obviously Kimberly had sent Pippa a picture of her friends and written who was who on the back.

Mandy sighed unhappily. "Darn. We look like little kids in that picture. If you can recognize us all from that, then we've wasted a lot of time and money this summer trying to look more grown-up."

Pippa smiled and put the picture away. "Trust me. It's better to grow up on the inside than on the outside. Where's Marissa?"

"She went to pick up dinner," Kimberly told her.

Pippa nodded. "Great. I'm starved. I'm sorry I wasn't home when you got here, but I'm adding two new Surf Shops and a hotel gift shop to the chain, and I've had to spend a lot of time checking things out. Marissa's been a big help."

"Listen, Pippa," Kimberly began. "About Marissa . . ."

Pippa walked around the counter into the kitchen. She jerked open the refrigerator door and began taking out sodas for everybody. "She looks great, doesn't she?" Pippa put in, cutting Kimberly off before she could say anything nasty. Pippa put the sodas down and gave Kimberly a level stare across the counter. "I'm so glad to have *both* my nieces here," she said, emphasizing the word *both*. "I'm so glad that they *both* feel comfortable and welcome. And I know that you are *all* going to look out for each other so that I don't have to act like a grown-up and make you guys play nice. Right?"

The message was clear. We were going to have to put up with Marissa—or else.

It was a setback. No doubt. Here we were, planning on an all-Unicorn vacation—and now we had to include a nonstop-talking, braces-wearing, donkey-laughing, pushy seventh-grader.

I started to feel a little angry with Kimberly for not warning us.

But like I said before, one minute you're up in the sky and the next minute you're bumping along on some concrete. Things change. And when Marissa came in the door, whatever was in the takeout bag smelled like heaven. My anger disappeared, and I was flying high again.

One way or another, things would work out.

They had to. We were thousands of miles from home. On an island. What choice did we have? We could either work it out or start swimming.

We fell on the food like we were starving.

Right now I'm sitting on a window seat looking out at the ocean with a big moon reflected on it after a dinner that was not to be believed. I don't know what they put in the food here in Hawaii to make it taste so good.

I'm so full, it's hard to imagine that I won't sink to the bottom of the ocean tomorrow.

Pippa had ordered us some kind of fish that was baked with nuts and fruit and rice. I had two helpings, and I don't even like fish.

We had mango ice cream for dessert, and there was enough for everybody to have as much as they wanted.

During dinner Pippa didn't tell anybody to sit up straight or stop talking with their mouth full. She didn't say one word about the music that Mandy put on—which was giving even *me* a headache. Pippa didn't even say anything when Ellen had a fourth helping of ice cream. I can't think of one single adult I have ever met who could watch somebody eat four bowls of ice cream and not have to warn them that they would get sick or that their teeth would fall out.

This trip is definitely going to be the best Unicorn trip ever. The only blot on the landscape is Marissa.

Marissa babbled about surfing and equipment all through dinner. She helped out in some of the Surf Shops, so now she thinks she's a big surfing expert. You'd think *Marissa* was the surfing champion instead of Pippa.

After dinner Kimberly showed us some of Pippa's trophies. She's won, like, every surfing contest in the world. And she doesn't brag at all.

If I had won all that stuff, I'd never shut up about it.

And if *Lila* had won all that stuff, she'd have billboards up all over California announcing what a big deal Lila Fowler was. Too bad the only thing she could brag about at dinner was her "high-school boyfriend."

She was obviously trying to impress Pippa by telling her about Wiley. Pippa asked a lot of questions about him, but I could tell she was only doing it to be polite. Only an egomaniac like Lila would believe that Pippa, a world surfing champion, would actually *care* that Lila Fowler was dating some ninth-grader nobody ever heard of.

Ha!!!

Uh-oh! I hear Rachel and Lila whispering. They're motioning me to come down to their room. I don't like the look on their faces. Something's up.

More later . . .

Four

Dear Diary,

The minute I walked into Rachel and Lila's room, I knew there was going to be trouble.

Everybody was there except Kimberly and Marissa.

"OK, clearly Kimberly has no influence over Pippa at all," Lila said. "I can't believe her. She got us here under false pretenses. She knew there was a possibility that Marissa was going to be here, but she didn't say one word because she knew we wouldn't come. I would never have left Wiley if—"

I groaned and rolled my eyes. I couldn't help it.

"What?" Lila demanded, real defensive. "What's your problem?"

"Would you cut the *Romeo and Juliet* act?" I begged. "You can live without Wiley Upjohn for a few weeks."

"You don't understand," Lila said in this soap-opera voice. "You've never had a serious relationship with a guy in high school and—"

I pretended to play the violin.

Lila reached into her pocket and whipped out a platinum credit card. "That does it. Marissa may be Kimberly's cousin, but she's not mine, and I personally don't intend to let her ruin what's left of my vacation." Lila walked over to the phone. "I'm booking myself on the next plane out. Who's with me?"

Her hand hovered over the receiver.

I felt a huge lump rise in my throat. Did this trip mean so little to Lila that she would walk out on it over something so small? "Guys! Please!" I said. "This may be our last summer together," I reminded them. "Am I the only one who cares?"

Mandy chewed her fingernail. She's the nicest Unicorn of all of us—including me. And like I said, she's very sentimental. I waited for her to say something. Something in defense of Marissa. Or Kimberly. Or the trip. But she didn't. She looked torn. Like she might decide to leave with Lila.

I looked around the room. There were a lot of stony faces. I hadn't realized until then just how much influence Lila was starting to have over the club. It was scary.

Finally it was Ellen who spoke up. "Lila," she said in a small voice. "We just got here. I don't want to go home."

I probably shouldn't have been surprised. As

ditzy as Ellen is, she's not the follower she was in the sixth grade. After a year as president she's become more confident about being her own person.

"I don't want to go home either," Mandy blurted out—like she felt OK about saying it now that Ellen had. Her eyes were on Lila, though.

Lila shot a look at Rachel. "What about you?"

Rachel's eyes flickered. Rachel was the newest member of the Unicorn Club. Belonging to the club meant a lot to her when she first joined. Did it still? "I'm staying," she said after a long pause.

I felt glad about that. But in a way it made me sad because being a Unicorn meant more to Rachel than it did to Lila. And Lila had been a Unicorn much longer than Rachel.

"Please stay, Lila," I said softly. "Please."

I couldn't believe I was begging Lila to stay. Over the years we've had lots of fights. Most of the time I'm thrilled to see her split.

Not this time, though. I had the feeling that if she left now, it would be for good. We'd never put our friendship back together.

Finally Lila's shoulders relaxed. She frowned and stuffed the card back in her pocket. "OK. OK," she said—like she was doing us all some big favor. "I'll stay. But somebody's got to keep that conceited little pit bull called Marissa under control."

I couldn't help thinking that Marissa wasn't any more obnoxious or conceited than Lila.

Still, I went over and sat down next to Lila. "So what if Marissa tags along with us?" I asked in a gentle voice—not ugly or anything. "What difference can it make?"

Lila lifted her chin. "If we were back home, I'd say we were committing social suicide by letting Marissa hang with us. She's a dork. Period."

"But we're in Hawaii," I reminded her. "Nobody will ever know."

"Jessica's right," Mandy said.

Ellen nodded.

"So we're all cool?" I asked.

"What about Kimberly?" Rachel asked. "What do we say to her?"

"Let's try not to make a big deal out of it," Mandy said. "I'm sure Kimberly feels weird enough. And we don't want to get her into trouble with Pippa. Let's try to be nice to Marissa."

So, Dear Diary, the storm seems to be over for now.

After the meeting I came back to the room I'm sharing with Kimberly and Marissa. They're in Pippa's room, so I've got a little privacy to get caught up here.

Oops! Just heard Pippa's door open. I can hear Pippa's deep laugh and Marissa's giggle. Kimberly is laughing too. I guess they had a little private family reunion.

Here they come.

Bye.

THURSDAY, 8:30 A.M.

Dear Diary,

By the time we went to bed last night, I was feeling totally good. The cot was really comfortable. When I lay down and turned out the lights, I could see a ton of stars out my window. I fell asleep looking at them.

I must have been asleep a long time, even though it seemed like one minute I was looking at stars and the next minute I was watching the sun come up.

I don't usually wake up early, but I guess I was just so excited to be in Hawaii that I woke up on my own. And there was this incredible bright orange-and-pink ball rising in the sky.

It just made me want to sit up and shout, *Good morning!*

So I did.

You can imagine how happy this made Kimberly. Not very. Kimberly is very grumpy in the morning.

But Marissa sat straight up in bed. Then she got up and jumped from her bed onto Kimberly's and from Kimberly's bed onto my cot. "Incredible!" she crowed, looking out at the sunrise.

Then she practically fell on my stomach. The two of us started laughing so hard, the cot began to jiggle and then . . . *wham!* . . . it collapsed right underneath us.

Both of us thought that was hilarious, but Kimberly just grunted something extremely un-complimentary about sharing a room with hyenas and pulled the cover up over her head.

Since Marissa and I were the only two people inter-ested in getting up, we decided to go into the kitchen and fix a big breakfast for everybody. But Pippa was al-ready up and dressed and frying bacon in a huge pan.

Bacon is the world's best alarm clock. It wasn't long before the smell had lured everybody out of bed and into the kitchen. Marissa made fresh-squeezed orange juice while I manned the toaster.

It was a great breakfast, and I took mine out on the balcony. It's still a little cool, so that's why I'm working on my diary instead of my tan.

I figure in another hour it'll be time to hit the beach. Inside the condo I can hear everybody talking and laughing. I can hear Marissa giggling. For some reason it's not bothering me today. In fact, I think she's kind of funny.

I have a feeling that everything is going to work out just fine.

SUNDAY, 1:00 P.M.

Dear Diary,

I can't believe it's been three days since I wrote anything. But there's been so much going on, I haven't had time. Today is a rainy day, so I'm finally getting a chance to catch up.

Hold on while I read what I last wrote.

Note to myself: Don't *ever* write the words *everything is going to work out just fine.*

The minute you do that, you're toast.

After breakfast that first day Pippa took us on a drive around the island. She's got this fabulous Suburban, and we all packed in. We drove through Kapiolani Park, which extends from Waikiki Beach to Diamond Head. Then we went (at my request) to the Ulu Mau Village, where there's a model of a Hawaiian chief's village. I thought it was totally interesting. I think Ellen and Mandy did too, but they wouldn't admit it because Lila and Rachel were both acting like it was a big snooze. I don't know if they acted that way because seeing the village was my idea or because they had both been there before—twice.

Nobody snoozed, though, when we went to the Royal Mausoleum, which has the remains of five Hawaiian kings and one queen, Queen Liliuokalani. She was the last monarch in Hawaii and a very great lady. And she wasn't just a queen; she was a composer too. She wrote "Aloha Oe." I've heard that melody all my life, but I never knew where it came from.

We stopped for dinner at a little roadside seafood place. Everybody was so tired and sleepy by the time we got home that we just fell into bed.

The next morning Pippa had stuff to do, so we decided to hit the beach.

We took our towels, sodas, sunscreen, magazines, hats, sunglasses, sandals, wraps, snacks, and floats down to the beach and set up shop.

Marissa spread out her towel next to mine.

That was OK.

Marissa said she really liked me a lot and felt very comfortable talking to me.

That was OK.

Then she told me that because she liked me so much and felt so comfortable talking to me, she was going to give me some advice.

That's when I knew I was in trouble.

"Jessica," Marissa said, "have you ever thought about low lights? It would really bring down that yellow in your hair."

"My hair isn't yellow," I said, trying not to sound insulted. I don't like to brag, but everybody always says that my hair is one of my very best features. And here was this . . . this . . . this . . . *seventh-grader* . . . giving me advice about low lights.

I heard Lila give a little snort of laughter on the other side of me. Like she thought it was funny and I was getting what I deserved for sticking up for Marissa the night we got here.

Marissa sat up a little and stared at me hard. Then she nodded. "You're right. I think it just looks too yellow because of that lipstick. That's not a good pink on you."

Lila rolled over. She was laughing so hard, I could see her shoulders shaking.

"You should trade lipsticks with Lila," Marissa went on. "The apricot she wears is all wrong with her coloring, but she would probably look good in that pink."

Lila quit laughing. She rolled over and scowled at Marissa. Then she stood up with a little huff and dusted the sand off her legs. "I'm going in," she said haughtily.

"By yourself?" Marissa asked in this grown-uppish *reminding* voice.

Lila paused. Even though her tone had been annoying, Marissa was right. All of us knew better than to go in the ocean without a buddy.

Lila looked at me—obviously hoping I would volunteer to go in with her. I pretended to be absorbed in my book. It was windy, and I really wasn't ready to go in.

Nobody else volunteered to go either.

"Guys!" Lila urged. "Come on!"

"I'll go into the ocean with you, Lila," Marissa chirped, like she had no clue that Lila couldn't stand her. She hopped up and dropped her sunglasses on her towel.

"There's a bathing suit shop at the end of the beach," Marissa said, turning toward us. "We could all walk down there in a little while and maybe Ellen could find one with boy-cut legs."

"I don't want one with boy-cut legs," Ellen argued.

Marissa frowned. "But you should. It would take an inch off your thighs. Yours too, Jessica," she said with a smile.

My jaw fell open. Ellen's thighs don't need an inch off them, and neither do mine. Our thighs are just fine. Was Marissa actually telling us we looked . . . *fat?*

I could see Lila's mouth twitching. Like she was trying very hard not to laugh again. "Marissa," she said, egging her on. "We're so lucky you're here. Obviously we need all the help we can get."

Marissa didn't pick up on the sarcasm at all. "Oh, I love to help people," she said seriously. "That's what friends are for. And I'm so happy we're all going to be friends."

Then she punched Lila on the arm. "Race ya," she said—like she was about ten. She tore down to the water.

Of course Lila was too dignified to race. So she

made a big show of not hurrying. She stretched, put her hair in a ponytail, and then turned to me. "You might want to put on a hat," she drawled. "The sun is really going to bring up that yellow in your hair."

I threw my paperback at her just as she turned and ran toward the water, laughing.

Rachel sat up and watched Lila and Marissa diving into the waves. "Kimberly . . . ," she began. "About Marissa . . ."

Kimberly was lying facedown. "There's nothing I can do," she said, her voice muffled. "I don't want to hear it."

Rachel sighed and lay back down. "Well," she said. "At least there's one good thing about Marissa."

"What's that?" Mandy asked.

Rachel started to laugh. "She didn't tell me *my* thighs looked fat."

"Ha-ha," Ellen said.

Everybody settled down to their books and magazines. I couldn't help taking my little mirror out of my tote and checking my face. Was my lipstick really too pink?

Then I told myself to stop worrying. I was an eighth-grader. Why was I worried about what some little seventh-grader with braces thought?

Low lights! She didn't know what she was talking about.

It was while I was looking in the mirror that I saw the *cute guy!*

He and some other guys were coming down to

the beach behind us. Feeling kind of like a spy, I watched him. What a babe!

He was tall and had straight brown hair down to his shoulders. His eyes were bright blue. He was laughing at something one of his friends had said, and he had these superwhite teeth.

My heart started thumping like crazy.

That's when I realized that Mandy was talking to me.

"Jessica!" she was saying. "Hello? Are you there?"

"Yeah . . . I was just . . ."

"Deciding where to put the low lights?" she teased.

"You're hilarious." I put down the mirror. "What did you say?"

She leaned over Rachel and whispered, "I said that there are a lot of cute guys around."

"I noticed."

"Pippa said there's a club down by the pier. It's teens only tomorrow night. Let's go."

"Sounds like a plan," I said, already trying to decide which of my fabulous new sundresses to wear.

I looked back over my shoulder, wondering what the cute guy and his friends were doing. They were only a few yards away, and miracle of miracles, he looked right at me.

His blue eyes met mine, and he smiled.

Then a Frisbee came sailing toward him, and he dove for it. He didn't look back at me. He was too busy running around and laughing.

But we had made eye contact. It was a start.

After a little while the cute guy and his friends

left the beach. But we stayed and spent the rest of the day swimming, bodysurfing, and hanging.

I kept hoping the cute guy would come back, but he never did.

By late afternoon everybody was pretty pooped. We decided to go take showers and then find burgers. I decided to take one last walk along the beach to see if I could spot the cute guy.

Marissa offered to walk with me.

At first I wasn't too thrilled to have her with me. But then as we walked along she leaned over and found a sand dollar. Whole. Unbroken.

I told her I'd never found a whole one. Ever. And that she was lucky.

She told me she *was* lucky. Lucky that the Unicorns had come.

Then she handed me the sand dollar and told me it was a present. She said that she was going to remember this summer forever—because it was the first summer she had had friends.

I didn't know what to say. I felt flattered but also guilty. Because I know the other girls really don't like her. They're only tolerating her. They aren't really her friends, and neither am I.

But I couldn't tell her that. So I just thanked her and said it was really nice of her to give me the sand dollar.

Then I felt even guiltier. Because I knew that if *I* had found the sand dollar, I would have kept it.

I heard somebody calling us and saw Kimberly waving from the balcony. It was time for dinner.

Hold on. The phone is ringing.

It's Wiley. For Lila. She's giving me this dirty look like she wants me to get out of the alcove so she can sit here and have some privacy while she talks to Wiley.

No way.

Let her call him back on her stupid little mobile phone, which she has to have with her every single moment of the day in case Wiley needs to tell her something urgent, like that it's raining back in Sweet Valley.

Now she's whispering.

Now she's giggling.

Now she's whispering and giggling while looking at me so I'll think she's talking to Wiley about me.

I'm not going to give her the satisfaction of watching her put on a big show, so I'll finish this later.

Five

◇

Dear Diary,

Later . . .

(Lila spent about two hours talking to Wiley. Their phone bills are going to be huge.)

Now that she's off the phone, she's sitting in the living room draped over the sofa, looking languid and lovelorn. Watching her is really making me feel ill, so I'm turning the other way while I write.

Back to the story . . .

OK. So the next day (which was yesterday) we were all going to the teen club.

The entire day was devoted to primping, starting the minute we got up. Fingernails. Toenails. Hot oil treatments. Plucking. Steaming. All that stuff is very time consuming, and before we knew it, it was five o'clock and time to start the serious dressing part of the evening.

Marissa went into the bathroom around five and *would not* come out. I thought Kimberly was going to have a total conniption. Finally Kimberly decided to get ready in Pippa's bathroom and I went in and shared Rachel and Lila's bathroom—which annoyed them, but I really didn't have any choice.

When Kimberly and I got back to the room, Marissa was *still* in the bathroom.

"Think something's wrong?" Kimberly asked.

"Maybe we should call the fire department," I suggested. "Maybe she's stuck in the tub."

Finally the door opened and out she came.

"Ta-da!" She twirled out of the bathroom like a ballerina. "How do I look?"

"You look great," I said, and I meant it. I was floored. Her hair was on top of her head in a messy updo, and she had on a short sundress with a flippy skirt in a big, bold, black-and-white check.

"I think I look like I'm in at least the ninth grade," she said proudly.

Kimberly, who was standing in front of the dresser trying to get the clips into her hair, turned around and rolled her eyes at me.

I rolled my eyes back.

"I'm going to show Pippa." Marissa flounced out of the room and down the hall to Pippa's room.

Modesty is not Marissa's best sport. All afternoon, while we had been primping together, she had been getting more and more full of herself.

Everyone was getting pretty sick of her. But when Lila had raised the possibility of leaving Marissa at home while we all went to the club, Kimberly vetoed it. Pippa wouldn't stand for it, she told us.

I wasn't too thrilled about having Marissa come to the teen club with us, but I wasn't as bugged as Lila. I was in too good a mood to be bugged by anything. I hadn't seen the cute guy again, but somehow I had a feeling he would be there.

"Whooooa!" Rachel said, coming into our room. She looked at me and turned her thumb up.

I had on my new lime green dress with butterfly cutouts on the back. My hair was down and loose, and I had long swinging earrings made out of abalone that picked up the green of my dress. "You look gorgeous," I told Rachel, returning the compliment.

Rachel had on white silk pants with a bright red silk shirt tied at the midriff. It was all very sixties Cher-glam. Rachel pretended to model and then flopped down on the bed. "Hurry up!" she yelled to Lila and the others.

"*I can't,*" Mandy shouted from the bathroom across the hall. "*I'm having a hair emergency!*"

Ellen came in, laughing. "Mandy's pink extension fell out. Has anybody seen it?"

That broke us up, and we all started looking around the apartment for it. Finally Lila found it out in the hall. She came back in holding it between her fingers with her nose wrinkled. "I think it got stepped on, and there seems to be something gummy stuck to it."

"Ewwwww," we all chorused.

Mandy went over and examined the damage, then she dropped it in the wastebasket. "Oh, well," she said with a sigh. "At least I've got the orange and green ones."

"If I were you, I'd get rid of those too," Marissa piped up. "Nobody wears those things anymore," she said in this obnoxious woman-of-the-world tone of voice.

"Marissa!" Kimberly said sharply. "Why don't you keep your opinions to yourself?"

Marissa didn't look fazed. "Hey!" she said. "If you can't trust your friends to tell you the truth, who can you trust?"

"We *are* Mandy's friends," Lila said. "And we happen to like the extensions."

"You're kidding," Marissa said, like she couldn't believe we all had such terrible taste.

"*Let's gooooo!*" Rachel shouted.

And that was the end of that.

Everybody ran around finding their purses and stuff. I noticed Mandy was looking at herself in the front-hall mirror while we waited for the elevator. "They look great," I whispered. "Don't worry."

Mandy gave me a weak smile. She looked really pretty in a vintage raspberry silk sheath and matching sandals. She pressed her lips together and tweaked her extensions. "That kid is starting to work my nerves," she said.

"That kid is starting to work everybody's nerves," Ellen muttered.

"Can't you *do* something?" Lila asked Kimberly.

"Like what?" Kimberly wanted to know.

Before Lila could answer, Marissa came out of the apartment all smiles and talking a mile a minute as usual.

"The teen club is such a cool place," she said breathlessly. "Everybody goes there—all the kids from this stretch of the beach and all the kids whose parents are staying in the hotel on the other side of the cove. Don't worry if you don't know anybody. I'll introduce you to all the people I know and—"

Good thing the elevator bell rang. I thought Lila might just strangle her.

We walked to the teen club. Marissa managed to totally irritate everybody before we even got there.

But she was sure right about the club. It was definitely *the* place to be. Wall-to-wall kids. The music was hammering, and the dance floor was packed.

I was really excited that so many people were there. But I was on a mission: I had to find the guy from the beach.

Marissa sort of elbowed her way through our little crowd. "Follow me," she ordered.

So we did. She seemed to know her way around the place, and we scooched along behind her. Somewhere in there she disappeared. The rest of us didn't know what to do, so we just kept going until we came out on the other side of the crowd and found ourselves in an open area that faced the beach.

There was no back wall, and the crowd spilled out onto this big deck that extended all the way into and over the water.

There was a juice bar set up on the deck, so we

headed for it. The guy behind the bar was a babe with black hair, long on top and shaved up the back and sides. He had earrings in both ears and a killer smile. He winked at me and said, "I already know what you want."

"No, you don't," I said with a laugh.

"OK," he agreed. "But I know what you should have. You need a drink to go with that dress. Let me make it for you. First one's on the house." He reached for the blender and started pouring all kinds of stuff in the canister.

"What's it called?" I asked, trying to watch what he was doing. His hands and wrists moved so fast, I couldn't keep track. He was like a magician. Bottles and chunks of fruit seemed to appear and disappear like magic.

He dropped some ice cubes into the mix. "What's your name?"

"Jessica."

"Hi, Jessica. My name's Carl, and this drink is called a Jessica Hawaiian Iced Jade Surprise." He hit the button and the whole thing exploded inside the blender. Two seconds later he switched it off, whisked off the top, poured the mix into a tall glass, and handed me a drink that was the *exact* same green as my dress.

Rachel clapped. "That is so cool. Can you make me something to match my blouse?"

Carl opened his arms. "You're looking at the primo blender-drink artist of the Western world. Of course I can make a drink to match your blouse." He pretended to study the color. "That is one gorgeous red," he commented, reaching for a bottle.

Half a minute later Rachel was sipping something tall, icy, and crimson.

"Where's Marissa and Mandy?" Kimberly asked as the bar guy went to work on something for Ellen.

"I think we lost them," Rachel said. "Ohmigosh, look!"

I looked and nearly fell over. The bar guy had actually made a drink that was *yellow and red striped*—just like Ellen's tank top.

We all burst into applause, and he took a dramatic bow.

That's when Marissa found us. Mandy was behind her. "Hi, Carl!" Marissa said.

The bar guy straightened up from his bow and gave Marissa a wide smile. "Look who's here," he said happily. "How ya doin', sweetheart?" Then he saw Mandy. "Hi," he said, sort of quietly.

"Hi," Mandy replied. Then she flushed slightly pink.

Naturally Marissa ignored the obvious chemistry going on between Mandy and Carl. She flashed us a big metal smile. "I see you met my friends. Guys, this is Carl. When he's not working here, he works for Pippa at the Surf Shop."

"Busy, busy, busy," he joked, managing to tear his eyes off Mandy.

"What do you do in the shop?" Rachel asked.

"Actually, I'm a clerk and surf instructor," Carl answered, turning back to Mandy, even though it was Rachel who had asked the question. "If people buy their equipment from the shop, they can book lessons with me."

"Can you make a drink to match my dress?" Marissa challenged.

We all laughed since her dress was black and white.

"How about I make a drink to match your eyes instead?" he suggested—which I thought made him sound very gallant.

After he had handed a drink to Marissa, he smiled at Mandy. "I knew there was a reason I stocked up on raspberries."

Mandy smiled shyly while Carl made her a frozen raspberry drink to coordinate with her outfit. I love a man who can accessorize.

By then there was a line forming behind us. So when we all had our drinks, we had to move on— even though I could have spent the whole night talking to Carl and watching him make those drinks.

"I think he likes you," I heard Rachel whisper to Mandy as we moved toward the dance floor.

Mandy giggled. "Really?"

Before anybody could say anything else, Lila gasped. "Oh, no!"

"What?" I asked.

"Oh, nonononono!" Lila groaned, turning quickly so her back was to the crowd. She pulled me slightly aside. "There's Peter Feldman."

"Who?"

"Peter Feldman. He goes to Sweet Valley High. Correction. He *rules* Sweet Valley High. And he knows Wiley." She pointed to this guy who was standing over by the rail with some older-looking kids.

"So let's go say hi," I suggested.

Lila grimaced. "Are you kidding? With Marissa around? No way. I don't want him to see me hanging with her. Let's just try to get past them and keep from being seen."

"Lila! If he's here, we're going to run into him sometime!" I argued.

But Lila had already scooted away into the main part of the club. Rachel, Ellen, Marissa, and Kimberly were standing by the opposite rail, looking down at the water.

I started to go over to them but decided I'd rather go into the club and see the sights.

Inside the club it was dark and really crowded. I walked around, smiling at people who looked friendly. But I was really looking for the guy I'd seen earlier. I had a feeling about him. Like I was just supposed to see him again.

I was still looking all around when somebody tapped me on the shoulder. I turned and sucked in my breath. It was him. The cute guy from the beach. He had on khakis and a bright yellow polo shirt. With his long hair and big blue eyes, he looked like the perfect combination of clean-cut and hip. My kind of guy.

"Hi!" he shouted. "I'm Jason Landry. I saw you on the beach yesterday."

"I saw you too. My name's Jessica Wakefield," I shouted back.

"Do you want to dance, Jessica Wakefield?"

"Sure!" He took my hand, and we somehow

found a place on the dance floor. We moved back and forth, but it was so crowded, people kept bumping into us.

After about the third time he backed into somebody and I did too, he just threw up his hands—like he was giving up—and then he put his arms around me so that we were dancing close instead of apart.

It was the most romantic thing that had ever happened to me. He put his arms around me like it wasn't any big deal at all, and I felt totally comfortable putting my arms around him.

We danced—swaying back and forth—until the music was over, then we left the dance floor. He took my hand and pulled me toward the deck. "Let's go outside so we can talk," he shouted.

I nodded and followed him. As we walked outside we passed the whole group. Lila's mouth opened slightly, and Rachel put her hand over her mouth to hide her smile. Ellen gave me a thumbs-up.

I felt just totally great. I—Jessica Wakefield—had snagged a babe. "That's better," he said, leaning back against the rail. "I can hear again."

"Are you here for vacation?" I asked him.

"Yes and no. I spend every summer here. My folks are divorced, and my dad lives in one of the condos on the beach. I've been coming for so many years, it feels like a second home. I've got a whole set of friends here. Activities, all that stuff. During the school year I live in Vermont. What about you?"

"I'm here visiting," I said. "From California."

Just then two other guys came up. "Hey!"

"Hey!" Jason said. "This is Jessica. Jessica, this is Rafe and Larry." Jason grinned at me. "Didn't you have some friends too?" he asked me.

I laughed, turned, and motioned the gang over.

They came over, giggling. Everybody introduced themselves, and pretty soon even more guys found their way over. Almost all of them were staying near Pippa's condo.

Everybody was talking, laughing, and flirting. Then all of a sudden, along came Marissa.

She went right up to Jason and said, "Hi. I saw you playing Frisbee yesterday."

"I saw you too," he said with a smile. "You're a good bodysurfer. You took some big waves."

Marissa smiled and giggled. "I guess it comes naturally. I'm in the surfing business."

"Oh, brother," I heard Kimberly sigh.

How typical. Marissa had helped Pippa out in the surf shops, and now she was acting like they were *her* shops.

"So how does everybody know each other?" Rafe asked.

I started to answer, but before I could even get a word out, Marissa jumped right in. "We're all friends," she told him. "We're having a house party. I got here early so I could scope out the scene and get ready to be the hostess with the mostess."

Kimberly glared at Marissa, but she wasn't paying any attention. Even if she'd seen Kimberly glaring, it wouldn't have fazed her. It would have taken an elephant to squash Marissa.

I didn't blame Kimberly for being mad. Marissa was making it sound like it was *her* house party and we were all *her* guests and *her* friends.

Then, as if she hadn't been nervy enough, she turned to Jason and said, "Oh! This is my favorite song in the whole world. Come on. Let's dance." Then she grabbed his hand and practically dragged him into the club where the dancers were.

I couldn't believe it. I couldn't believe that here I was getting this great thing going with Jason—and Marissa—*Marissa with her stupid braces and hee-haw donkey giggle*—had just kidnapped him.

"He's just being nice," Mandy whispered to me. "Don't get bent."

I tried to relax. Mandy was right. Obviously Jason was a really sweet guy. It was probably clear to him that Marissa was younger and didn't really fit in with our crowd—so he was going out of his way to be nice to her.

Handsome *and* a good personality. My favorite combo.

The next thing I knew, the whole gang was headed for the dance floor. All of us girls and about six guys, including Rafe and Larry.

We joined Marissa and Jason in the middle of the floor. Once we started dancing, it was impossible to figure out who was dancing with who. It didn't matter. We just danced in one big group and had a fabulous time.

Finally after about an hour Jason opened the collar of his shirt, pushed back his hair—which was damp with sweat—and took my arm. "Let's get some air," he shouted.

I was ready. Not only was I hot; the muscles in my legs and arms were turning to rubber. We went out on the deck and over to the juice bar. Carl wasn't there anymore. There was another guy behind the bar, and Jason got us a couple of orange juices.

"Let's walk on the beach," he said.

We walked down the wooden steps to the sand. I took off my sandals and hid them under a log. He took my hand, and we walked to the water.

"Marissa's got a great house party going," he said.

I was just about to set him straight on the Marissa thing when he put his arm around my shoulders. "You know, I really like the way all of you have so much fun together. At my school, hanging in a group can be impossible. Some of the kids are such backstabbers, it's scary. The minute you start talking to someone, he'll start bad-mouthing the others. You guys don't do that. Marissa had nothing but nice things to say about you and everybody else."

I shut my mouth and groaned inside. What could I say now? That Marissa was a little pest and we couldn't stand her? And have Jason think that we were worse than the kids back in Vermont? I think not.

So I just smiled and changed the subject. "Tell me about your friends."

The water came up and lapped around my ankles, cooling me off. We started walking along, kicking up little sprays of water. "Rafe comes every summer—like me. Both his parents live here. His dad was transferred here by his company, but Rafe wanted to stay at his school back home, so he boards there during the school year. Larry is Rafe's cousin, and he's here to visit for the summer. The rest of the guys are sort of a pickup crew. You know, guys that are here with their families for vacation or visiting relatives. They're all nice. That's one good thing about being here during the summers—there's no shortage of people to hang with. For the past two summers I've been a camp counselor, but this year I'm taking the summer off to have fun. I love hanging out in a big group of people."

He snapped his fingers. "Hey! I'm going camping with my dad for a couple of days, but I'll be back Wednesday. Let's have a beach party Thursday night. We could make a bonfire and cook out. Play music and dance on the beach."

"Sounds great! What can we bring?"

Jason and I walked back to the club, planning who would do what. The guys would bring soda, ice, hot dogs, and buns. We would bring dessert, CDs, and a boom box. We'd all meet just before the sun went down to gather wood for the fire.

I took another moment to retrieve my sandals from under the log, and by the time we got back to the club, everybody was out on the deck. Jason and

I told them the plan, and they were psyched.

"Wait a minute," Kimberly said. "I'm not sure Pippa's got a boom box."

Marissa held up her hand. "Leave it to me," she said in this know-it-all voice. "I've got connections."

"Who?" Kimberly challenged.

Marissa gave her a Cheshire cat grin. "Carl! He keeps one at the shop. He said I could borrow it when my friends came. And now here you are."

She turned and stared directly at Jason, who looked impressed.

Believe it or not, it made me jealous.

It also made me determined that at the beach party, I was not going to share Jason with Marissa.

Marissa needed to learn that she was a seventh-grader. She was a kid. She could get away with some things, but not with everything. Such as dancing and flirting with *my* guy.

And so, Dear Diary, that brings us up-to-date.

A lot of good stuff is happening. But there's been a lot of stress and turmoil too. So I'm not going to sign off with any predictions about how wonderful things are going to go at the party. I don't want to jinx it.

Six

◇

Dear Diary,

Unbelievably, I'm actually starting to like Marissa. When she's not cranked up to hypergab, she's a lot of fun. She knows a lot of jokes. She asks everybody questions about themselves. And she loves hearing us talk about Sweet Valley Middle School. It's like she just can't get enough stories about the school and the clubs and the people.

That's really how we started to be friends. Marissa loves hearing stories about me and Elizabeth. And I like to tell them. I'm missing Elizabeth. A lot. Talking about her makes me feel closer to her even though she's a million miles away in the rain forest somewhere.

Marissa and I were sitting at the breakfast table laughing about one of those stories this morning when the phone rang. It was Wiley, for Lila.

The whole time Lila was on the phone, she kept giving me funny looks—like she was sizing me up. It was really starting to irritate me. So I turned my back on her.

Then Pippa came in. She had on a black vinyl shirt and low-cut blue jeans. She looked fantastic—but not like any grown-up I knew.

I couldn't help giggling. I could just hear Mr. Haver yelling, *"Nuts!!! She's nuts!!!"*

I tried to picture my mom in an outfit like that. No could do!

Anyway, Pippa asked Marissa and me if we wanted to run over to the Surf Shop with her. Marissa said she would go, but I was happy hangin'. Besides, I wanted to get caught up on my diary.

Lila was still talking on the phone, and I could see that Lila's phone fixation was working Pippa's nerves big time. Even though Lila was on her mobile and not Pippa's phone, the point was that Lila was being rude. When Lila was on the phone, she ignored everybody. She didn't say "good morning," "good night," "hello," or anything else. She didn't come to the table if we were eating. When Lila was on the phone, the rest of us might as well have been invisible.

But the worst part was that she wanted us all to be quiet. If we made any noise or interruption, she gave us dirty looks and shushed us.

Pippa and Marissa were on their way out, and Lila didn't even acknowledge they were leaving. She didn't wave or mouth the word *good-bye*. She just kept murmuring into the telephone like she and

Wiley were exchanging national secrets or something.

So Pippa marched over to the sofa where Lila was sitting and leaned over the back of it so that her long hair hung over Lila's head like a curtain.

Lila let out this little croak of surprise.

"Good-bye, Lila! Good-bye, Wiley!" Pippa shouted. "No! No! Don't get up. I wouldn't want to interrupt you." Then giggling like Marissa, she threw back her head and ran out the door.

I cracked up. I'd never seen an adult correct somebody's manners in such a hilarious way.

Lila still didn't appreciate it, though. She took the phone and stomped out of the room.

Half an hour later Kimberly came and told me we were having a meeting in Lila and Rachel's room.

I took what was left of my raspberry tea and followed her down the hall to the back bedroom. Lila, Rachel, and Ellen were all sitting there, looking really serious. So serious, I actually got worried. "What's wrong?" I asked. "Is somebody hurt?"

Lila shook her head. "No. But I talked to Wiley. He said that he's already starting to get invitations to some of the Welcome to Sweet Valley High parties."

"Goody for Wiley," I said. "What's that got to do with us?"

Lila folded her arms. "If you could cut the sarcasm for two seconds and let me finish, I'll tell you."

"Listen to her," Rachel said. "This is serious stuff."

"Wiley said that there are a lot of cute ninth-grade guys who don't have dates. And while they're not thrilled with the idea of taking an eighth-grader, they might be willing to ask an eighth-grade girl—*if*—she *measured up*. Know what I mean?"

I did. And I felt butterflies of excitement in my stomach. Actually going to high-school parties with high-school guys was just . . . I couldn't even think of words to describe it. And the best part was that it would *kill* Steven. He *loves* making me and Elizabeth feel like underlings. He'd just eat his heart out if I actually wound up at a high-school dance with a guy who might even be on the basketball team with him.

Suddenly I felt really bad about all the things I'd written about Lila in my diary. She didn't have to set all this up for us. She could have been the only Unicorn at the high-school parties and then gloated about it until we wanted to kill her.

For Lila Fowler, this was the ultimate generous act.

"I don't think we'll have any problems measuring up," I told her, sitting down on the bed. "We look great. All of us. We've got the hair. We've got the clothes. We've got the personality and the poise. We totally measure up."

"There's a problem," Mandy said in a flat tone.

"What?"

"Marissa," they all said at once.

Rachel looked at me. "I'm betting that the beach party is going to be huge."

"So?"

"So it means that Peter Feldman will probably be there," Lila explained. "Wiley says Peter Feldman has very high standards. If Peter's at the party, he'll see us with Marissa. And Marissa will probably collar him and tell him how the Unicorns are all her very best friends, and Peter will think we're the Nerd Patrol. By the time we get back to Sweet Valley, we'll be total laughingstocks. Believe me, Wiley's friends won't want to hang with the Unidorks."

I felt really torn. I resented letting Wiley Upjohn tell me who I could or couldn't hang with. And I was really starting to like Marissa. On the other hand, I didn't want her ruining my chances of social success in the eighth grade.

"So what can we do about her?" I asked. "Pippa made it pretty plain we have to include her."

Kimberly nodded. "Yeah. Pippa made it clear we have to include Marissa. But what if Marissa didn't want to hang with us?"

"Huh?"

"We're going to make *her* drop *us*," Rachel explained.

"How?"

Ellen giggled. "We have a plan."

When she told me about the plan, I had mixed feelings about it. But I realized if I didn't go through with it, I'd wind up dateless in eighth grade.

So tonight Operation Ditch Marissa goes into action. We will, of course, keep you informed as this story develops.

TUESDAY, 10:00 A.M.

Dear Diary,

Now, short sheeting isn't the worst thing in the world that could happen to you. But it's nothing you want to deal with on a regular basis. So when Marissa climbed into bed last night—and discovered she'd been short sheeted—we laughed and told her to get used to it. We told her that the Unicorns *loved* practical jokes, and we played them on each other all the time.

She laughed and tried to be a good sport about it. But when we turned off the electricity in the condo (Rachel found the circuit breakers) while she was trying to remake her bed—she got upset and went running to Pippa. (Pippa was already asleep, which is why she didn't notice the unusual power outage.)

Pippa appeared with a flashlight. "What's going on?" she asked sleepily. "Marissa said you guys screwed up her bed and turned off the electricity." Pippa didn't sound angry. But she didn't sound very amused either.

"It was just a joke," Rachel said. "We didn't mean to upset her." Rachel's tone somehow managed to sound concerned while also implying that if Marissa weren't such a baby, Pippa's sleep never would have been disturbed. That Rachel—she's good.

Pippa took the flashlight out into the utility room, found the circuit box, and flipped the appropriate switches. The lights came back on. After that, Pippa found another sheet for Marissa. She handed it to Kimberly. "Fix Marissa's bed tomorrow morning, will you, Kimberly?"

"Where is she?" Kimberly asked.

Pippa pressed her lips together. "She's going to sleep in my room tonight. We'll talk more tomorrow. OK?"

We all went back to our rooms. "Think Pippa's mad?" I asked Kimberly.

Kimberly flopped down on her own bed. "Probably not. She's probably more irritated with Marissa for waking her up than she is with us. But we've got to be careful. We can't look like we're singling Marissa out for the treatment."

This morning Kimberly and I went into action. *"Kimberly!"* I yelled, pretending to be mad as I chased her into the living room.

Kimberly ran into the living room, jumped over the couch, laughing hysterically, and "hid" behind Ellen.

"What's going on?" Ellen asked.

I held out my hairbrush. "Look!"

"What happened?"

"Kimberly cut all the bristles off!" I yelled.

Kimberly snorted. "That makes us even," she said. "Remember the time you put peanut butter in the toes of my shoes?"

Rachel threw up her arms. "Sometimes I am so sorry I joined this stupid club! *When* are you guys going to outgrow these practical jokes?"

"Never," Ellen told her with a big grin. "They're waaaay too much fun."

I flopped down on the couch like I was too tired to chase Kimberly anymore. And Kimberly came out of "hiding." She smiled at Pippa. "You wanted to talk to us?"

Pippa stood in the kitchen behind the counter, holding a cup of coffee. She took a sip and stared at us all, like she was thinking hard. Trying to put last night's short-sheeting episode into perspective.

Finally she smiled. "I just wanted to tell you guys to leave the circuit breakers alone. I've got some computer equipment in my room, and you could mess it up. Now I want everybody to get dressed. We're going on an outing. All of us. I'll tell Marissa." Pippa left the room, and we all froze for a moment, then we silently pumped our fists.

The plan is working.

I've been ready for the last twenty minutes. But Marissa's still in the bathroom getting ready, and so is Lila.

I wonder where we're going? Pippa won't tell us. But she's standing in the living room, yelling at us all to, "Move it! Move it! Move it!"

TUESDAY, 8:00 P.M.

Dear Diary,

Did I say Pippa was cool?

Talk about an understatement.

Not only does she have a Suburban, several surfing trophies, and her own chain of surfing shops, she has *a plane!* And a pilot's license!

We went out to this little private airport where a bunch of small passenger planes were lined up ready to take off. Over to the side there was a small building that looked more like a hut. We went inside, and Pippa introduced us to Mr. Hajit.

Mr. Hajit is a pilot, and he flies people from island to island. Pippa's plane only seats four, so she had arranged with him to help her transport us all to Maui for the day.

Kimberly, Marissa, and I went with Pippa. Everybody else flew with Mr. Hajit.

I'd never been on a little plane before, and I expected to be scared. But I wasn't scared a bit. I felt even safer than I do in a big plane. I guess because we were flying close enough to the ground that we could see everything—all the islands and roads and houses. It felt more like gliding than flying.

I couldn't help imagining what would happen if the engine blew out. In my imagination, we were so light that we circled down like a gull and skimmed along the surface of the water.

We landed at another little airport on Maui. This guy named Steve met us with a van.

Pippa is going into the gift shop business, and she's opening a store in a fancy hotel on Maui. Steve's dad is managing the shop for her. They're still getting it ready.

I'm beginning to think it's Mr. Haver who's "nuts." Pippa's no surf bum. She's a big-time businesswoman.

Anyway, Steve is sixteen and very Polynesian looking and has straight black hair down to his waist, practically. He wears it in a loose braid. Talk about gorgeous!

Lucky Kimberly. She got to sit between him and Pippa in the front seat. He and Kimberly hit it off great. She even asked him to the party Thursday night. Unfortunately he said he had to work. He and his dad are doing some renovation.

Anyhow, he drove us all over the island. Maui is made up of two volcanic mountains. Between them are lots of sugarcane and pineapple plantations.

Steve had brought a picnic lunch, and we ate it in the Haleakala National Park—where we saw the crater of an actual volcano. It's inactive—so we didn't have to outrun any lava—but it was very cool.

We spent the whole day driving over the island. Up and down winding roads and mountain peaks. I've never seen so many gorgeous and romantic views.

After that, we stopped by the hotel where Pippa's shop is going to be. Talk about plush! Wow. It's a high-rise with sprawling grounds and gardens.

The gift shop area is still full of lumber and dust, but I can see that it's going to be very nice when it's finished. We met Steve's dad. He looks a lot like Steve—but older of course.

He seemed very happy to meet Kimberly and Marissa. When Pippa said they might be coming back to help out, he smiled and said he would be delighted to have them. Then he made a point of taking Kimberly on a tour of the renovation and showing her stuff. He even asked her advice about whether or not to use mirrors as shelves.

I could tell Kimberly was flattered to be asked for her opinion.

Soon it was time to be heading back. Steve drove us all to the airport. Mr. Hajit was waiting for us. We all climbed back in the little planes and went buzzing back to Oahu. As I looked down I wondered what it was like in the old days, when people got from island to island in long canoes.

We got home about an hour ago. Kimberly is sitting on the balcony, staring at the water with a very introspective look on her face.

Ellen and Rachel are trying to figure out if Larry and Rafe are interested in them. And if they are— which guy is interested in which girl?

And Lila is . . . what else? . . . on the phone with Wiley.

She's hanging up. She's motioning for everybody to meet her in her room.

Bye.

TUESDAY, *9:40 P.M.*

Dear Diary,

Lila just called us into her room and gave us the rundown on the big social lineup taking place back in Sweet Valley.

Come September, it's going to be parties, parties, and more parties. Wiley is talking to some of his friends about us as potential dates. But Lila says he's very nervous about this middle-school/high-school dating thing.

According to Lila, all hinges on making a good impression on Peter Feldman. He's leaving Hawaii and going back to Sweet Valley soon. And he's going to be running the orientation program for the new freshmen!

It's absolutely, positively "imperative" (according to Wiley) that we get the Peter Feldman seal of approval. Which means phase two of Ditch Marissa goes into action tomorrow.

Kimberly held up her hand. "Hold it," she said. "I'm beginning to think this is not the greatest idea."

Lila frowned. "What do you mean?"

Kimberly bit her lip. "It's just not a great idea. Marissa's not so bad. She hasn't done anything to us. And Pippa's been really cool. I don't want to let her down."

Rachel nodded. "Kimberly's right. Pippa's really rolled out the red carpet. If she wants us to include Marissa and be nice, isn't that the least we can do?"

Mandy nodded, and so did Ellen.

Lila stood up and put her hands on her hips. "Kimberly, you're going to be in high school this coming year. Don't you see what that means? It means you have more at stake here than any of us! We all have a year to make our reps before high school. You've got *maybe* a few weeks. Remember, you're going in there alone. No backup. We won't be there to sit with at lunch. We won't be there to talk to between classes. If Janet thinks you've slipped—she won't even acknowledge you exist."

Kimberly swallowed nervously.

It was brutal, but everything Lila was saying was true.

I looked at Ellen, Mandy, and Rachel. Their eyes were big and scared.

"So I'm telling you guys," Lila continued. "If you want to be players in September, you're going to have to do it my way."

I watched Rachel's face. Rachel is just as rich

and spoiled as Lila. Just as used to getting her way. She was the one Unicorn who could usually be counted on to challenge Lila.

She looked like she was thinking things over. Trying to decide whether or not to let Lila push her around.

"Do I have to remind you guys that only one of us here is dating a guy in high school?" Lila asked. That was the clincher, and she knew it.

Rachel blew out her breath. "OK. Tell us what to do."

"Just act cool. Like you're not impressed with anybody or anything. We've been there, and we've done that. We're over it. We're over *everything*. Got it?"

Mandy chewed a nail and nodded. So did Ellen.

"That's just dumb," I said. "Jason and his friends didn't dance with us because we looked bored. They danced with us because we looked friendly."

"Friendly is for dorks like Marissa," Lila snapped. "And speaking of Marissa . . ."

Forget it. I just can't write anymore. Maybe I'll feel different about everything tomorrow.

WEDNESDAY, 7:00 P.M.

Dear Diary,

I woke up this morning feeling sick to my stomach. At breakfast I said I didn't feel too good and didn't want to go. Lila gave me such a dirty look, I changed my story and said I felt great and was ready to roar.

The plan was that we were all going to go snorkeling at Malaka Cove and play another "joke" on Marissa.

Pippa said she was going to be out most of the day and wouldn't be back until late that night. But she said it was fine for us to go snorkeling at Malaka Cove as long as we stayed together, and she wrote down directions for how to get there.

On the bus to Malaka Cove, Marissa sat next to me and talked nonstop. It was a long bus ride, and sitting next to Marissa made it seem even longer. The bus was cold too. They must have had the air-conditioning turned up full blast.

Finally we got to the cove. We all took off our cover-ups and shoes and laid them on our towels. Then we put on the masks and fins and headed out into the water.

I'll say this for Marissa. She's irritating, but she is a really good swimmer. She's very brave too. She checked out stuff that I was way too chicken to approach.

I wish I were a better writer so I could describe everything I saw. When I read this diary twenty years from now, I'd like to be able to remember how beautiful it all was. Schools of fish like flower gardens swam around us. Their fins were like angel wings—so clear and graceful and delicate. They had personalities too. Some of them were quick and excitable—like squirrels. Some were slow and looked very bored—like they saw snorkelers every day and didn't think it was any big deal.

I was having such a good time looking at the fish and the coral, I forgot about what was happening back on the beach. So when Marissa and I swam back to the shore and walked up to get our stuff, I was almost as surprised as she was to see that her cover-up, towel, and shoes were gone.

Then I remembered.

The others were already on the beach toweling off and getting their stuff together.

"Where's my stuff?" Marissa asked Rachel.

Rachel looked surprised, like she had no idea what Marissa was talking about. "What stuff?"

"My cover-up," Marissa told her. "My shoes. My towel. All my stuff."

Rachel shrugged. "I don't know. I haven't seen it. Lila? What about you?"

Lila toweled her hair. "Nope. Haven't seen them." The tone of her voice made it clear that she couldn't care less about the whole situation.

Marissa was starting to scamper around in circles, looking at the ground like maybe her stuff would turn up in a clump of grass or behind some driftwood. "Guys! This is serious. Where is my cover-up and towel? I need my shoes."

Nobody expressed any concern. Nobody expressed any surprise. Nobody expressed any sympathy. In fact, nobody said a word.

Finally Marissa got it. She froze for a second. Then her eyes went from one face to the next. "You guys hid my stuff, didn't you?"

Lila opened her eyes really wide. The picture of fake innocence. "Why would we do that?"

Marissa gave Lila a weak smile. "I don't know. But can I please have my stuff back?"

"We don't have your stuff," Rachel said, buckling

her sandals. "It's getting late. Let's go, or we'll miss the bus."

Everybody started walking up the beach to the road. Nobody looked back. We acted as if we didn't care if Marissa was with us or not.

"*Guys!*" Marissa shouted. "I can't leave without my stuff."

Nobody paid any attention.

"Why are you doing this?" Marissa shouted, her voice breaking. "This isn't funny."

"Think she's getting the message?" Rachel asked Mandy.

"I think she's getting it," Mandy answered.

Marissa came running up behind us, her arms folded across her chest, barefooted and in her bathing suit. "If you guys don't give me my stuff, I'll . . ."

The bus pulled up right then. The door opened, and everybody got on. Marissa hesitated outside the bus, shivering. The bus driver frowned. "Come on, kid. Are you getting on or not?"

Marissa came running up the stairs, and Kimberly dropped some coins into the box for her.

Everybody sat down. Marissa started to sit down next to me, then she stopped. She gave me a hurt, angry look and threw herself into the seat across the aisle.

She turned her face to the window and didn't say one word on the way back. The only thing I heard was the sound of her teeth chattering in the cold.

I felt bad. But then I pictured her grabbing Jason's

hand and dragging him toward the dance floor. I wasn't about to let that happen at the beach party.

I didn't feel bad after that.

When we got back to the condo, Marissa stormed into our room, shut the door with a slam, and locked it.

"Oh, well," Kimberly said. "We can use the bathroom in the hall to shower. She can't keep us locked out forever."

We all took showers, changed into shorts and T-shirts, and found some hamburger meat in the fridge.

"Should I make one for Marissa?" Rachel asked, starting to make the patties.

"Yeah," Kimberly told her. "If she doesn't want it, I'll eat it. I'm starving."

I actually wasn't. I had a heavy feeling in the pit of my stomach. I pictured Marissa in the bathroom, sobbing her eyes out.

I was beginning to wish we hadn't done it. I was beginning to think I might even go into the room and apologize. I was beginning to think that Marissa wasn't nearly as bad as I thought.

But then Marissa came out of her room.

Her eyes weren't red. She didn't look like she had been crying. In fact, she looked like she had just spent the last two hours primping. Her hair was clean, and she'd styled it with hot rollers. Her makeup was perfect, and she had on a cute outfit. "OK," she said. "I just want to tell you guys that I am sooooo sorry."

Huh? I thought. We all looked at one another.

Marissa rolled her eyes upward, like a movie star accepting an award, and then let out this breathless little laugh. "I don't know what my problem is." She smacked her head. "I'm just dense, I guess. There I was all mad and worked up, when I should have been thrilled to death."

I looked at Lila. Lila looked at Mandy. Mandy looked at Ellen. Ellen looked at Rachel. And Rachel looked at Kimberly. Kimberly looked at me, and I shrugged.

Marissa ran over to me, threw her arms around me, and kissed me on both cheeks. "Thank you so much!" she said. "This is the best thing that has ever happened to me. I should have known. I mean everybody *knows* that hazing is part of club initiation."

She twirled around and flopped into a chair. "I can't believe it. It's a dream come true. *I'm a Unicorn!*"

I thought Lila might just faint right there and then. But all she did was give Marissa a thin smile.

I was wondering who was going to burst her bubble when the door opened and Pippa came in. "Hi! We got through early, so I came on home. How was Malaka Cove?"

Marissa jumped up, ran over to Pippa, threw her arms around her neck, and cried, "Oh, Aunt Pippa. Congratulate me. I'm a member of the Unicorn Club."

Pippa looked over Marissa's head at Kimberly and gave her a proud smile. "That's great," she said quietly. "Really, really great. I'm proud of you." But when she said it, she was looking at Kimberly—telling Kimberly she was proud of *her.*

Kimberly flushed. Talk about an awkward situation.

"I think I'm going to take a walk," I announced.

And I escaped.

I probably walked about two miles down the beach. It was nice being by myself—which I really didn't understand at all. I usually don't like to be alone.

But I had some thinking to do.

It had seemed so important to me that we all be together on this trip. I had been looking forward to having a last blast with my best friends before eighth grade started. But we weren't having as much fun as I thought.

The problem was Marissa, I decided. Marissa was bringing out all our old, mean, competitive, manipulative personalities. We were all so afraid that her nerditude would rub off on us, we were acting like sharks.

The sun was going down, and I realized that if I didn't get back to the condo, the others might get worried. So I turned around.

When I got back, I found everybody sitting around the living room, pretending to be busy.

Right now Pippa is stretched out on the sofa, watching a movie.

Marissa is sitting on the floor between Ellen and Rachel with a bowl of popcorn. She's chattering away about what a great time we're all going to have at the beach party.

Mandy is in the kitchen, organizing the cereal boxes or something.

Every time I look at Lila, she gives me this series of eye, mouth, and head signals.

Now she's doing the same thing to Kimberly.

Now Kimberly is doing it to me.

Looks like they're trying to tell me to meet them in Lila's room. Should I pretend I don't understand?

Oh, well. What's the use? Might as well go in and get it over with.

Seven

Dear Diary,

I Here's what happened when Kimberly, Lila, and I finally managed to have a little private chat—in Lila's bathroom.

"Well?" Lila demanded. "What are we going to do?"

Nobody spoke up.

"She thinks she's a Unicorn!" Lila yelled, like she was reminding us that we had an emergency on our hands. "Tomorrow night there are going to be about a hundred kids on this beach, including Peter Feldman! And if I know Marissa, she's going to be sure she tells everyone that she's a Unicorn."

"OK! OK! Chill out!" Kimberly said. "I know it's a problem. I just don't know what to do about it."

"I vote we just tell her flat out she's not a Unicorn," Lila said.

"No way," Kimberly said.

"Why not?" Lila demanded.

Kimberly sighed. "Look. Pippa's cool. But she plays hardball when she has to or when she feels like something's not fair. She refused to accept a trophy once because she thought one of the judges had penalized another surfer for no good reason."

"So?"

"So she's already told me how proud of all of us she is for including Marissa. If we act like jerks and tell Marissa she's not a Unicorn, Pippa might get peeved enough to put us all on a plane back home."

"OK, then," Lila said. "What if the 'club initiation' somehow prevented her from going to the beach party tomorrow night?"

Kimberly lifted her eyebrows. "What do you have in mind?"

Lila reached into her bag and pulled out her little mobile phone.

"Who are you calling?" I asked.

"Janet," she answered.

For once I was glad she had that stupid mobile phone.

THURSDAY, 4:00 P.M.

Dear Diary,

Tonight's the night.

Party night!

Right now I'm resting up for the big event.

Today we all went shopping. I bought a salad bowl for Mom and Dad, a poster for Steven, and a beautiful book on Hawaiian history for Elizabeth.

I bought myself a new bathing suit—with boy-cut legs. *No, not because I thought my thighs looked fat.* I got it because it's a totally cool style and it was on sale.

The mall looked pretty much like the malls at home except that it opened onto outside courtyards in various places and all these exotic birds came flying in and out.

It was totally cool. Like shopping at the zoo or something.

The only cloud on the horizon was the Marissa thing. Janet had come up with a plan for a "prank" that would keep Marissa from attending the party.

But I felt bad about doing that to her. And frankly, I was sick of Lila and Lila's rules.

So I volunteered to play a major role in the "prank." But my plan was to make sure the "prank" didn't happen.

After we shopped, we had lunch at this little café with an outdoor patio. I was thinking about Jason and how I couldn't wait to do some close dancing—when suddenly Marissa piped up.

"I can't wait to see Jason," she said. "I wonder if he's been thinking about me as much as I've been thinking about him."

I had a hard time keeping my jaw from hitting the table.

What was she talking about?

Then she talked about how she planned to dance the night away with Jason! *My guy!*

My memory suddenly flashed on the moment

when she asked Jason to dance and dragged him onto the dance floor—leaving me in the dust! Well, that did it. I *couldn't* let Marissa get between me and my guy! Not when I'd been looking forward to this party for *days*. So I decided to follow the plan *as written*.

I made an excuse to come back to the apartment a little earlier than the others. When I got back, I slipped green food dye into Marissa's toothpaste. Here's how:

I snipped the end off an empty tube of lip gloss. Then I washed out the tube and shoved the nozzle down into Marissa's toothpaste tube. That way I could use the empty lip gloss tube like a funnel. I poured the green dye into the lip gloss tube and squeezed it down into the toothpaste. Then I squished the toothpaste around in the tube so that it would be more or less an even color.

When Marissa brushes her teeth, she's going to look like she's been munching a seaweed salad.

All I know is that I wouldn't go to a party with green teeth for a million bucks. We're betting Marissa won't want to either.

Uh-oh!

I just heard the front door.

They're back.

THURSDAY, 11:30 P.M.

Dear Diary,

Well, what can I say? Things didn't exactly work out the way I had planned.

The somebody I'd heard coming in wasn't the

gang. It was Pippa. She asked me where everybody was, and I told her they were still out shopping. She said OK and that she had to make some phone calls.

I think it was the first time I had ever been in the condo alone with just one other person. No TV. No music. No conversation in the background.

Suddenly I realized it was so quiet, I could hear sounds I'd never noticed before—like the hum of the refrigerator and the birds chirping outside the sliding-glass door to the patio.

I could also hear Pippa talking on the phone in her room.

It sounded like she was talking to Marissa's mom. She was saying stuff like, "Oh, yeah, Marissa seems to be fitting in just fine. The other girls are being very friendly." Things like that.

Then I heard her say . . . "Yes. A practical joke or two. No. No. I don't think there will be any more. . . . No, I don't think they're picking on Marissa . Well, I'm just not going to let them. . . . How? . . . I'll take them all straight to the airport and send them home if I have to. . . . I don't care what Jack and Anne think." (Jack and Anne are Kimberly's parents.)

Then she went on. "I've never cared whether they approved or not. I do what I think is right. And if the girls can't accept Marissa, they'll have to clear out. . . . Well, if their parents don't like it, they should teach their kids better manners."

Kimberly had told us that Pippa had pretty definite ideas about how people should behave. People like us. If we didn't play by her rules, she would have no problem kicking us out.

Did I want to be packed up and sent home?

No way.

Not only would it make the Unicorns look bad, it would make *Pippa* look bad. Mr. Haver had said he didn't think she could handle us. He had said she would wind up sending us home.

I didn't want him to be right.

Besides, I still had spent hardly any time with Jason!

I was on my way into the bathroom to throw the toothpaste away when the others came in. Before I could say anything, Lila turned to Marissa. "Marissa. I can really smell those onions you had for lunch."

Marissa giggled and put her hand over her mouth. "I'm going to go brush. I don't want onion breath tonight of all nights."

"Mind if I use the bathroom first?" I asked, trying to head her off so I could throw out the booby-trapped toothpaste.

But naturally Marissa's such a kid, she thought I was challenging her to some kind of race. She broke into a giggle and ran in front of me, cutting me off. "You're first—after me!" she yelled. The next thing I knew, she had run into our bathroom and shut the door with a bang.

I drifted back into the living room. Everybody sort of pretended to be busy putting their things away. Lila had a strange, crooked smile on her face.

Suddenly we heard this wail come from the direction of our room.

Ellen started to laugh and had to cover her

mouth. She ran out of the living room and into the back bedroom. Mandy followed her.

Two seconds later Marissa was standing in the middle of the living room. "Look at me!" she wailed. "Look at me!"

She took her hand away, and Rachel choked on a laugh. Marissa's mouth and teeth were stained green.

"It won't come off!" she cried. "What is it? What did you do to my toothpaste?"

"You said you wanted to be a Unicorn," Lila reminded her.

Marissa's face was just . . . I can't describe it. I could see she wasn't sure what she was supposed to be feeling. Happy or sad? Humiliated or proud?

"How do I get this off?" she asked in a small voice.

"You don't," Lila snapped.

Marissa's face crumpled. Her mouth began to tremble, and her head began to shake. She looked just miserable. "I can't go to the party looking like this," she cried, tears running down her cheeks.

Marissa threw herself facedown on the sofa and sobbed. Great big heaving, heartbroken sobs. "I've tried to be a good sport," she wailed. "Why are you doing this to me?"

Lila looked like she could hardly keep from laughing.

I wasn't laughing. I was on the verge of crying too—I felt really awful. I knew what it was like to have people be mean to me because they thought it was funny. I knew how cruel the Unicorns could be.

Janet had made me do things like carry her books

for her. And kiss Randy Mason! (Ugh!) And partici-
pate in mean jokes on people like Lois Waller.

And I had hated it!

Suddenly I felt furious. With Janet. And with
Lila. With Rachel and Kimberly. And even Mandy.
What did we think we were doing?

I looked up and saw Pippa standing in the living
room. She was obviously furious. And when she
looked at Kimberly, her expression turned to disap-
pointment. Then to disgust.

"What happened?" she asked quietly.

Marissa sobbed that she had tried to be a good
sport, but now she had green teeth and couldn't go
to the party.

Pippa leaned over, put her hand on Marissa's
back, and whispered to her to go into *her* room.
Pippa's room.

Marissa threw us all a hurt look, then got up and
ran into Pippa's room, slamming the door behind her.

Pippa told Kimberly to get everybody into the
living room. That she had something to say to us
and would be back in a couple of minutes. Then
she went after Marissa.

My heart sank. I knew that she was going to tell us
all to start packing our bags. I didn't want to leave. I
didn't want our last summer of the Unicorns to end—
especially not like this. I didn't want to leave Jason. I
didn't want to go home feeling like a Janet Howell
clone. I didn't want Mr. Haver to say *I told you so.*

All this was going through my head in about
two seconds.

Then I had an idea. A way to save the situation. I ran into the bathroom, grabbed the toothpaste, and brushed like crazy until I had a big green smile myself.

I ran back out into the living room just as Pippa was clearing her throat. She looked at me and did a double take.

Everybody looked at me and did a double take.

Rachel's mouth fell open.

"Your turn, Kimberly," I said, trying to sound totally relaxed. I grinned at Pippa. "We do this at parties back home. It's kind of a California joke. I guess we should have explained it to Marissa."

Pippa shook her head. "I never heard of this."

"Oh, it's a new thing," I said, giving Kimberly a long, steady look.

I could tell from Kimberly's pale face that she knew we had come very close to getting booted. "Yeah," she said, playing along. "It always makes people laugh. Kind of a conversation starter, you know? We're *all* going to the party with green teeth." Kimberly clamped her hand on the fleshy part of Lila's arm. "Aren't we, Lila?"

Before she could argue, Kimberly and I had shoved Lila into our room and shut the door.

"Never," Lila whispered. "Not in a million years."

"If you don't," I said, "I will personally introduce Marissa to Peter Feldman and tell him that Marissa is your very best friend."

Her eyes snapped. "You wouldn't," she challenged.

"Oh, yes, I would," I said. I went into the bathroom,

grabbed the toothpaste, and plopped it into her hand. "In fact, if *everybody* doesn't have green teeth by the time we leave, I'll do it."

Lila looked at me like she just hated me. "This is . . . blackmail."

I nodded. "That's right."

Lila took the toothpaste and marched out of the room. I plastered a big smile on my face and went back out into the living room.

Marissa was standing in the kitchen. Pippa had made her an ice pack to hold over her eyes. "I'm sorry," she said, her voice hoarse. "I know you guys think I'm a big baby. I shouldn't get so upset. You're just trying to be my friends."

"Well, you'd better go start getting ready," I said, trying to sound happy and perky. "We need to be out on the beach in another hour."

Marissa hiccuped and smiled—her braces and gums a big green mess.

Then I realized mine were a big green mess too.

That's when it hit me.

Lila was all worried about what Peter Feldman was going to think.

What was *Jason* going to think when he saw my green teeth???

(Note: I am turning into a pretty good writer, I think, because if this were a novel, that would be a perfect way to end this chapter. Sort of a cliff-hanger. I think I'll leave it there because I have to go to sleep. I'll finish the story about what happened tomorrow.)

Eight

Dear Diary,

It turns out that nobody is speaking to me today. They're not making it so obvious that Pippa or Marissa would notice. But they're giving me the silent treatment.

And guess what?

I don't care!!!

Why don't I care?

Here's why.

Before we went down to the beach party, Lila made everybody brush their teeth with the green toothpaste.

Then . . . she made them all promise they wouldn't smile in case Peter Feldman was there. She figured that if nobody smiled, nobody would notice that we had green teeth.

All things considered, she told them, it wasn't the worst thing that could have happened. According to Wiley, guys like girls who are distant and sophisticated. If nobody smiled, they would look very distant and sophisticated and probably have all the guys eating out of their hands.

We loaded up a big plastic laundry hamper with the bags of goodies and went down to the beach with our CDs and the boom box. It was still light. The sun hadn't even begun to set.

Everybody looked great. Marissa had on khaki shorts and a sleeveless blue denim shirt tied at her midriff.

Lila had on a bright blue bathing suit with a matching long skirt slit all the way up the side. She looked like she stepped right out of a magazine.

Mandy had on some baggy shorts and a halter top. Kimberly wore black shiny bicycle shorts and a bathing suit top that showed off her athletic figure. Ellen wore her bathing suit and cutoffs.

I wore my tie-dyed dress. I guess I was just feeling sort of defiant.

Anyway, when we went down to the beach, we could see about thirty guys and girls already gathered. A bunch of them were piling up driftwood for the bonfire.

We got closer, and I saw Jason.

Jason, Larry, and Rafe all came running over to help us carry our stuff.

We all just kind of mumbled "hello" and kept walking with our heads down—except for

Marissa, who grinned and chattered away.

Jason gave her a sort of funny look. But Marissa seemed oblivious—I guess she had forgotten all about her teeth. She giggled and began talking to Jason about our shopping trip. He asked her all kinds of questions, and she got started talking about her collection of carved animals.

Just as I was beginning to think Jason was going to spend the whole beach party talking to Marissa, Carl showed up. He had a couple of surfboards with him and invited anybody who felt like it to take them out.

"Hey, Mandy," he prompted. "Want to give it a try?"

Mandy looked up and smiled (with her lips together). But Lila gave her a little nudge, and Mandy's smile immediately disappeared. "No, thanks," she said, turning her back on him and walking over to where the drinks were.

"I do," Marissa shouted. She grabbed one of the boards and started running toward the waves. She jumped in with her clothes on and started paddling out.

Jason watched her go. "Wow! Marissa's really enthusiastic, isn't she?"

Carl, Kimberly, and a couple of other guys followed Marissa out into the surf. They looked like they were having fun. I couldn't help thinking Mandy had made a big mistake.

"Hey, Jason. How about you guys go see if you can find some more firewood?" Rafe said.

Jason nodded. "OK. We'll be back. Come on, Jessica."

I was hoping Jason would take my hand, but he didn't. Oh, well. The night was young.

"Let's walk down to the pier," he suggested. "We can collect wood on the way back. That'll give us a nice walk while the sun sets."

"Brilliant idea," I said, thrilled that this wood collection trip was sounding so romantic.

We walked about half a mile. At one point I turned and couldn't even see the group anymore. But as we walked, kids kept passing us on their way to the party. Lots of people had blankets and bags of food. Lots of them knew Jason and said hello.

Overhead, the sky was turning a gorgeous pink and orange as the sun began to set.

"It doesn't matter how many sunsets I see," he said. "They always amaze me." He put his arm around my shoulders.

I felt this shuddery feeling between my shoulder blades. Then I put my arm around his waist. I felt him turn slightly toward me, and my heart began to pound. Was he going to kiss me? He leaned toward me and—

Suddenly we were attacked by munchkins!

We broke apart as three little boys danced around us, whooping and hollering. I was sort of embarrassed and extremely annoyed.

Who *were* these little sand rats?

Jason's face was red, but he didn't look angry. He was laughing. The smallest one jumped up, and Jason lifted him up on his shoulders. The kid was so thrilled, he screamed.

Jason began to gallop.

"Me too! Me too!" the other two cried, chasing behind them.

Jason gave all of them a turn riding on his shoulders. Finally he swung the last kid down. Two of them ran off, but the third grabbed Jason's arm. "I want another ride," he demanded.

Jason shook his head. "Not now, Hal. Maybe tomorrow."

"Now!" Hal insisted, stamping his foot.

"No," Jason said gently but firmly. "It's time for you to go home. The sun is almost down."

Hal looked up at Jason's face, like he was trying to decide whether or not to throw a tantrum. Then he pointed at me. "Who's that?" he asked.

Jason gently pushed Hal's finger down and stooped so that he was face-to-face with Hal. "It's not polite to point," he whispered.

"I don't care," Hal said.

"Yes, you do," Jason said with a smile. Then he put his hands on Hal's shoulders and turned him to face me. "Hal, this is Jessica. Jessica, this is Hal."

"Hi," I said, flashing him my winningest smile.

Hal stared at me for a long time without saying anything. Then he made this horrible face and gagging noise. "Spinach mouth!" he groaned.

"Hal!" Jason said sharply. "That's not nice."

Ohmigosh!

I had *completely* forgotten about my teeth. There I'd been—all puckered up like I expected Jason to kiss me, and he'd probably been totally grossed out by the idea.

Hal stubbed his toe around in the sand. "I'm sorry," he muttered. Then he turned his eyes toward Jason. "I don't like her. Will you come and make a sand castle with me?"

Jason shrugged an apology at me and sighed. "I'm playing with Jessica right now. Why don't you go play with Rick and Jeffrey?"

Hal kicked the sand, obviously bummed. "I don't want to play with them."

"Why not?" Jason asked softly.

"Because they don't want to play with me."

"Why not?" Jason asked again.

"Because they don't like me. But I don't care because they stink. *And so do you!*" he yelled at me. With that, Hal turned and ran up to a beach house and disappeared.

"How do you know Hal?" I asked, trying not to look insulted.

"Hal goes to the camp where I used to be a counselor."

"The camp is in Hawaii?"

Jason nodded. "He's home this weekend because he takes medication for an illness and needs to see the doctor. He'll go back to camp on Monday."

"I feel sorry for his counselors," I said.

Jason flashed me a sideways glance, and I remembered that I was supposed to be the sensitive, caring type.

"They must miss him," I added quickly. "He's such a character."

Jason smiled. "Poor Hal. He's just one of those

kids who has a hard time fitting in. He can be a total pain. I don't know if he doesn't have any friends because he's a pain or if he's turned into a pain because he doesn't have any friends. But I figure, hey, maybe all it takes is one friend to break the cycle. So I'm trying to be that one friend. Listen, about that remark he made . . ."

"I guess I'd better explain about the teeth," I said, terrified of what he would think when he heard the truth.

I told him the story. Most of it. Not all of it. I just said that a couple of the girls had played a prank on Marissa and she had gotten upset. So we had all turned our own teeth green to make her feel better.

He just stared at me with these big, puppy-dog eyes. Shaking his head like he couldn't believe it.

"I guess we're not as nice as you thought we were," I said unhappily.

"No," he said. "You're not as nice as I thought you were. You're nicer." Then he kissed me. Unfortunately it was on the cheek. But it was a start.

After that, the night got better and better. We spent most of the beach party dancing or sitting together by the fire.

And guess who showed up? Steve. He talked his dad into letting him fly over with Mr. Hajit. Steve and Kimberly danced the night away. And Carl boogied with Marissa.

Mandy was nowhere to be found. Ditto for Lila, Rachel, and Ellen.

Know why?

Because they didn't stay for the party, that's why.

The others had gone back up to the condo even before Jason and I got back with the wood.

I was the last one of our group to leave the party, and I figured that everyone would have been asleep for hours by the time I came home.

Kimberly and Marissa had gone to bed.

But Lila, Mandy, Rachel, and Ellen were sitting up waiting for me when I came in. They looked like a bunch of gargoyles perched on a wall.

"Whose side are you on?" Lila demanded.

"What do you mean?" I asked.

"How could you do this to us?" Rachel asked, giving me a green-toothed snarl and pointing to her mouth.

I sat down. "I knew that if we didn't do something, Pippa was going to send us home. I heard her telling Marissa's mom so on the phone."

Lila folded her arms across her chest. "So?"

"So I don't want to go home," I protested. "Neither does anybody else. Right, guys?" I looked at Ellen and the others. But nobody said anything.

My heart started thudding. Uh-oh.

"Wiley says there are a lot of parties going on back home," Lila said. "Maybe we should all go back to Sweet Valley and—"

"No!" I yelped. "No way. I'm not leaving Jason."

Lila's mouth fell open a little. "Jessica," she said in this really superior tone. "Just because you've danced with somebody doesn't mean he's your boyfriend."

"He is too my boyfriend," I insisted. It was *almost*

true. He seemed to like me a lot anyway. And everyone was ready to do whatever Lila told them to do just because she had a boyfriend. Well, two could play that game.

"He kissed me," I told them. Technically this is true. Why muddy the waters with details?

Lila lowered her eyelids. "Yeah, right."

Mandy and Ellen chewed their cuticles like they didn't know what to believe.

"Personally," Rachel said, "I have a very hard time believing that any guy would kiss a girl with green teeth."

"I don't care what you guys think," I retorted. "If you'd stayed, you would have seen for yourself." (Boy, was I glad they hadn't.)

"Why would we have stayed?" Rachel asked. "Nobody even talked to us or asked us to dance. It wasn't like the teen club at all."

"They didn't talk to you or ask you to dance because you looked like total snots," I pointed out. "You guys didn't smile or talk to anybody."

"How could we smile with these green teeth?" Lila practically screamed.

There was a thumping on the wall. It was Pippa, signaling us to keep the noise down.

"Look," I said. "We can have just as much fun here as we would in Sweet Valley. Come on, guys."

I got, like, a zero-degree enthusiasm reading.

"Suit yourselves." I stood up and started to saunter out of the room. "But Rafe and Larry sure will be disappointed."

"What!" Ellen and Rachel both said at once.

"They like you," I said. "Can't you tell? They asked about you."

Rafe and Larry hadn't exactly asked about Ellen and Rachel *specifically*. But they had asked me where everybody was. So technically they had asked about them.

"OK," Rachel asked eagerly. "But who was asking about who?"

I shrugged. "I'm not sure. And I guess the only way to find that out . . . is to stick around and see what happens."

Nine

◇

SATURDAY, *3:10* P.M.

Dear Diary,

Even though people aren't talking to me, the balance of power seems to be shifting. Lila Fowler is no longer the supreme dictator. Everybody has a stake in staying now.

Kimberly likes Steve. Mandy likes Carl. Rachel and Ellen like Rafe and Larry (or maybe Larry and Rafe?). And I like Jason.

Usually it's Lila who's sitting by the phone waiting for it to ring. But today it's me. I just know Jason is going to call me and ask me out to lunch or something. And I cannot wait to see the look on Lila's face.

SUNDAY, *9:00* A.M.

Dear Diary,

Jason never called yesterday. I took four walks,

hoping to see him, and he wasn't on the beach. I'm trying not to get worried. Maybe he thought it was uncool to call so soon after the party. That's it. He'll call today for sure.

SUNDAY, 6:30 P.M.

Dear Diary,

It's almost dark. I haven't seen him, and he hasn't called. Lila has asked me six times where my "new boyfriend" is. Thankfully my teeth are no longer green.

MONDAY, 11:00 A.M.

Dear Diary,

I wish I had never come to Hawaii.

MONDAY, 3:00 P.M.

Dear Diary,

It's now been four days since the beach party. Jason never called, and I haven't seen him.

Today we went down to the beach and Lila almost had a cow because Peter Feldman—*the* Peter Feldman—actually came over and sat down with us.

He and Lila talked about all these people at Sweet Valley High, and Lila was name-dropping like they were all her incredibly close personal friends.

She was acting, like, *so* Marissa.

The rest of us felt kind of shy and nervous. It was one thing to flirt and giggle and goof with guys who you met in a club. It was another thing to flirt and giggle and goof with a guy who was a sophomore at Sweet Valley High.

If you made a fool of yourself, people back home would hear about it. So everybody was a little subdued.

Fortunately Marissa was out in the surf with Carl and Kimberly. He had wandered down with a couple of boards.

While I listened to Lila and Peter talking, I watched Marissa. She was lying flat on a board, waiting for a wave. After letting a couple go by she started paddling, getting her board into position.

The wave got bigger and bigger. Marissa managed to get up on her knees.

The wave started to curl.

Marissa started to stand.

I sat up and leaned forward. It looked like she might actually get up on her feet.

"She's doing it," I heard Mandy breathe. "She's doing it!" Mandy sat up too, watching.

Suddenly that wave looked about a thousand feet high. It was an unbelievable curl.

I realized I was holding my breath, watching her.

She was actually doing it! She was up on her feet, and she was *riding the wave!*

I jumped to my feet and let out this big shout. *"Yes!"* I screamed.

Mandy had jumped up beside me. She had her hands over her mouth. "Look at her!" Mandy choked. Her eyes were actually full of tears. I felt a lump in my throat too.

Marissa's arms were out, and she was teetering. But she was surfing. I couldn't help running down to the water. I heard Mandy's feet slapping the sand behind me.

Finally the board slipped out from under her feet. It flew up into the air, smacked the surface, and floated off.

A few seconds later Marissa surfaced, wiped her face, and looked around for the board. When she saw Carl grab it, she grinned and started jumping up and down and shrieking.

By this time I was about knee deep in the water. Marissa saw me and ran toward me and Mandy. "Did you see?" she yelled. "Did you see me surfing?"

"I saw! I saw!" I shouted.

"You did it!" Mandy shrieked. "You did it. You did it. You did it."

The three of us held hands and danced around—splashing with our feet to celebrate. Carl came over with Marissa's board and lifted his hand. Marissa smacked his palm.

He dropped the board and hugged her. "That was fantastic," he said.

"It *was* fantastic," Marissa agreed. "It was the most fantastic feeling in the world. I'm hooked."

Carl smiled at Mandy. "What about you, Mandy? Want to try?"

I hoped she would say yes. Her eyes were shining. She looked friendly and open. She looked like Mandy. She opened her mouth—

"Mandy!" Lila called. "Come over here."

In an instant Mandy's face had shut down. "No,

thanks," she told Carl. "I'm happy for Marissa, but I'm not really into surfing. You guys have fun." She turned back toward the beach.

I hurried to catch up. "Mandy," I whispered. "What's going on? I thought you liked him."

"Jessica! Think how stupid I would look if I couldn't do something and Marissa could," Mandy said. "I'd look like a total fool in front of Peter Feldman. Besides, Lila's calling me."

I felt like somebody had just dumped a bucket of cold water on my head. This was getting scary.

When we sat down, I could tell from Lila's face that Mandy and I had just made a major gaffe.

"Who is that girl?" I heard Peter ask Lila. He pointed to Marissa.

"That's Kimberly Haver's cousin," Lila said. "Nobody you would know."

Peter didn't seem to get that Lila was not interested in talking about Marissa. He leaned forward, watching her paddle back out into the ocean. "Looks like she's learning fast," he commented. "Surfing's hard. I've been trying for weeks and I can't stand up."

"Her aunt is a champion surfer," I volunteered. "Maybe it runs in the family."

Peter's eyes opened wide. "Cool! What's her aunt's name?"

"Pippa Haver," I said.

"I've heard of her," he said. "That's her niece? What's *her* name?"

If looks could kill . . . I wouldn't have lived to be writing this diary.

Lila was trying to put as much distance between us and Marissa as possible, and here was Peter Feldman wanting to know all about her.

"Her name is Marissa," I answered, ignoring Lila's glare. What was I supposed to do? Refuse to tell him her name?

He looked out at her and nodded. "She's cute. What grade is she in? Eighth? Ninth?"

"Something like that," Lila said, like she had no interest at all in talking about it.

Peter stared out at the water for a while, then he stood up. "I'll see you guys around. OK?"

"I'll tell Wiley you said hello," Lila told him brightly—just in case he had forgotten that she was dating Wiley Upjohn.

"Great," he said.

Then he started jogging away down the beach.

Lila bit her lower lip. Then she turned to me and said, "Let's take a walk."

MONDAY, 10:00 P.M.

Dear Diary,

Lila Fowler is insane with power.

It's hard to believe that this is the girl who has been my best friend since the second grade.

As soon as we started walking she said, "Jessica, I can make your life wonderful. Or I can make your life totally miserable."

I swear. That's exactly what she said. The dialogue could have come right out of some cheesy TV movie. I decided to call her bluff. "OK. Make it wonderful," I challenged. I folded my arms, tapped my foot, and pretended to look at my watch. "Well? I'm waiting. It doesn't seem any better to me."

"This is serious, Jessica."

"What do you want from me?"

"I want you to figure out whose side you're on. Stop sticking up for Marissa. Who's your best friend?"

"Gee, Lila. I was just wondering that myself."

Lila's face turned a little pale. "OK. I guess it's really hard for you to accept that I've matured lately. I have a boyfriend. I have an image that I have to protect. And you're too jealous to deal with it."

I felt my own face get kind of pale. She'd hit a nerve. I *was* jealous. But what did that have to do with Marissa?

"Don't you want to be popular next year? Don't you want to have dates? Don't you want to be cool?"

"Of course I do," I said. "What's your point?"

"My point is that if you don't stop acting like Marissa's big sister and best buddy, the Unicorns are going to go one way and you're going to go another."

My hands were shaking. A big lump rose up in my throat. I looked at Lila and I was filled with *rage*.

Who did she think she was—telling me who I could hang with and who I couldn't hang with? It was like having Janet Howell back in charge.

"Think about it, Jessica," she said in this real threatening tone.

She turned on her heel and started walking away.

I walked in the other direction. I was crying. I couldn't help it. I was so miserable. This trip wasn't turning out the way I wanted it to at all. Lila was acting horrible. And Jason hadn't even called me.

I had started out thinking that we wouldn't be having these problems if Marissa weren't here. But now I think we wouldn't be having all these problems if *Lila* wasn't here.

Maybe Wiley will call her and tell her he can't get along without her. Maybe we'll get lucky and she'll book herself a flight back to California and leave the rest of us alone.

Alone.

Boy, oh, boy. I am just bummed beyond words. Here I am with all my best pals—and I have never felt so lonely in my life.

Right now I'm sitting in the bedroom. Everybody else is in the living room, watching a rental movie. Lucky me. I can cry myself to sleep in peace.

Ten

Dear Diary,

This morning Kimberly and Marissa went off with Pippa to visit some family friends. Ellen, Lila, Mandy, and Rachel all went down to the beach.

I said I had some stuff to do and didn't go down with them.

"I wouldn't spend too much time waiting for Jason to call," Lila told me in a nasty voice as they left.

I sat down on the sofa with the phone in my hand. I was seriously considering calling my parents and asking them if I could come home early.

But I knew they would start asking me all sorts of questions. If I told them what was going on, it would sound totally lame. They'd tell me not to be ridiculous. They would tell me it would be rude to leave the house party. And they'd finish up by telling me that as soon as I got home, I'd beg them to send me back to Hawaii.

How can I tell them that something more important is going on? Something I can't really express.

I have this weird feeling that I don't know who I am. I don't feel like Jessica Wakefield anymore.

I don't feel confident or pretty or anything.

I don't feel comfortable with my friends. I don't like the way they're treating me. I don't like the way they're treating Marissa.

But I don't want to be on the outs with everybody. I don't want to wind up with geeky Marissa as my only friend.

Marissa has no clue what's going on. She still thinks she's being put through Unicorn membership initiation. She acts like we're best pals.

I hate her. I hate everybody.

I want to go home.

There's the phone.

Maybe it's Jason.

TUESDAY, 2:35 P.M.

Dear Diary,

It wasn't Jason. It was Pippa. She forgot to give some envelope to Carl and asked me to take it down to him at the shop.

I said I would.

TUESDAY, 9:30 P.M.

Dear Diary,

OK. Things are looking better. Not great. But better. The Surf Shop is at the very end of the beach.

There are benches out front where people can sit, drink sodas, and hang out.

I went inside the Surf Shop, and Carl was sitting behind the counter with another guy. Carl looked really glad to see me and introduced me to the other guy, whose name was Trey.

I gave Carl the envelope, which had some information about stuff they were supposed to order. They looked over the info and talked for a couple of minutes, then Trey got on the phone with the manufacturer.

Carl stretched and took some keys out of a drawer. "OK. It's quittin' time. I'm gonna catch some waves." He looked at me and cocked his head. "I can't believe that anybody as pretty and blond as you doesn't know how to surf."

I blushed. "I'd like to. I just never learned how."

"Want a lesson on the house?" he asked.

Under the circumstances, I couldn't really say no. This might sound really conceited, but I thought he might be flirting with me. Since Jason had done a fade and Mandy had made it clear her loyalties were with Lila, I figured, *Why not take Carl up on the offer?*

I had my suit on under my shorts, so I said sure.

Carl and I went outside and examined the boards that were leaning against the side of the shop. "These are for people to have fun with," he said. "Pippa figures that even if a few get broken or stolen, it's still good karma because somebody out there is surfing."

He found one for me and carried it under his

arm. We waded into the water. The waves weren't very big, and when we were about waist deep, he told me to get on the board and lie on my stomach.

I got on my stomach and paddled around for a little while.

As the little swells rose he told me to practice getting on my knees. I tried it and wiped out.

When I came up for air, Carl didn't laugh or make fun of me. He just smiled and told me to try it again.

I was starting to wish I hadn't accepted his offer of a lesson. I felt like an enormously clumsy dork.

He held the board steady while I climbed up on it again.

"Now just try to move with the board. You skate?" he asked.

"Sure," I answered.

"Well, this isn't that different. You just have to keep your balance over the motion."

We waited while some small waves passed underneath me, then Carl started saying, "Go . . . go . . . go . . ."

I paddled hard, trying to catch the wave as it rose beneath the board. Suddenly I was just into it. The wave, the board, and I were all moving together.

I got on my knees. I got one foot on the board beneath me. I was starting to stand when I heard this screech from the shore. I looked up and saw Marissa. She was jumping up and down, cheering. Pippa and Kimberly were with her. I was so surprised, I fell off the board with a big splash!

Dear Diary,

In our last entry, our heroine had just done a total and complete splashdown in front of Carl, Kimberly, Marissa, and anybody else on the beach who happened to be watching.

I guess I should be grateful nobody had a video camera.

Carl and I headed back to the shore, and when I got there, Marissa was all over me. "Jessica! I didn't know you were interested in learning to surf. I'll help you. Pippa's got tons of boards down in the basement and . . ."

Arggghhhh! Just what I needed—Marissa teaching me to surf. Luckily she went into the Surf Shack with Pippa and Kimberly. I had a few moments alone to try to regain a little dignity.

That's when I saw Kate and Larry!

Double arrggghhhh!

Could life possibly get any worse?

There I was, looking like a waterlogged geek. Mascara down to my chin. No lipstick. Hair plastered to my forehead.

Had they seen my ridiculous wipeout? And would they tell Jason?

They waved and hurried over. "Hey!" they said. "Learning to surf, huh?" Larry asked.

I tried to smile and make a joke. "Just trying not to drown."

It was kind of lame, but at least I was able to say something besides "uhhhhhhh."

I was so embarrassed. And I couldn't decide whether to ask about Jason or not. He hadn't called me, so it was pretty obvious he wasn't interested in seeing me.

"Listen," Rafe said. "Let me get your number. Jason wanted to call you, but he lost your number and he couldn't remember the name of the lady you're staying with."

"Jason wanted to call me?" I gasped.

Larry nodded. "Yeah. Jason was a counselor last year at a camp for special kids. Anyway, when he got home from the party, there was a message that some of this year's counselors had gotten food poisoning. They wanted Jason to come fill in. We went with him and came back today. Jason's staying on till tomorrow."

Suddenly life didn't seem quite so bleak.

In fact, it looked pretty darned sunny.

That was yesterday.

Which means Jason is coming back today.

All right!

WEDNESDAY, 8:40 A.M.

Dear Diary,

After breakfast I'm going down to the beach with the other girls. I didn't tell anybody about Jason. I'm just going to sit there and wait for him to come find me. If he's missing me the way I'm missing him, he'll sweep me into his arms, lay a big passionate kiss on me, and then *Lila Fowler can eat her heart out.*

I hope Peter Feldman is sitting there watching too so he can tell Wiley Upjohn that Jessica Wakefield has a boyfriend *who is taller than she is* unlike someone around here whose name happens to be Lila.

WEDNESDAY, 8:00 P.M.

Dear Diary,

Things didn't go exactly the way I scripted them, but they came close.

After breakfast we went down to the beach. I made sure I had on my new suit—*not because my legs are fat or even close to being fat*. It just made me look cool, that's all.

I lay on my stomach, wearing some new shades, and tried to ignore Marissa, who was lying next to me, reading from some book of surfing poems Pippa had on her shelf.

"Listen to this." Marissa cleared her throat.

> "A ball arcs through the air—
> Leaves no trace.
> A bird flies across the sky—
> Leaves no sign.
> I soar across the water—
> The sea swallows my evidence."

"Oh, give me a break," I heard Rachel mutter.

Marissa didn't hear her. She let out this long, dramatic sigh. "Oh, Jessica, once you've ridden the waves, you'll understand. I want you to have what

I had. I want you to experience what I have experienced. It's just indescribable happiness."

I saw Lila look at me over the tops of her sunglasses. "You asked for it," she sang under her breath.

I opened my magazine and ignored both of them. I pretended to read, but my eyes were scanning the beach, searching for Jason.

After a little while I spotted him. He was still pretty far off, walking toward us.

I closed my book and stood up. "I think I'll go get my feet wet," I said with an elaborate stretch.

I started toward the water, pretending I hadn't seen him. My heart was pounding, though. I kept imagining him getting closer and closer. It took a lot of self-control not to turn. But I was going to wait until he called my name.

Then I'd turn and let out a cry of surprise.

We'd run toward each other with our arms out.

The water would splash around our feet.

The sun would light up our hair.

It would be just like a shampoo commercial. Lila would gnash her teeth with jealousy.

I waited.

And waited.

And waited.

Finally I heard someone call my name.

But it wasn't Jason.

It was *Marissa!*

I turned around and there she was—standing with Jason and calling me over to say hello to him—

like she didn't get that he had come to see *me*.

Under the circumstances, I couldn't exactly go running toward him with my arms out. I walked over, trying to smile. But inside, I was wondering how to drown Marissa and get away with it.

I could feel Lila and the others watching. Trying to figure out if there was really anything romantic between me and Jason.

When I got to where he and Marissa were talking, he gave me a big hug.

That was something.

Of course, he might have hugged Marissa too for all I knew.

Jason put an arm around Marissa and an arm around me, and we all walked over to join the others. "Hi! Sorry to have been out of touch. We had sort of an emergency, and I left the island before sunrise the morning after the party."

Everybody asked him where he had gone, and he told them all about this camp for special kids. "Four guys are too sick to stay on. It looks like I'm going to be a counselor there for the rest of the summer," he said. "Rafe and Larry are going to fill in here and there. But I'll get three days off every weekend, so we'll definitely have some time to hang out."

He looked right at me when he said it.

SATURDAY, 7:05 P.M.

Dear Diary,

Well! Guess who's getting a little more respect these days?

Jason, Rafe, and Larry hung out with us for the past couple of days. We did a lot of group stuff. We played volleyball and took walks. Jason's dad, Mr. Landry, took us out on a boat one day.

Then it was time for them to go.

It's pretty clear now that Rafe and Larry are interested in Ellen and Rachel.

It's still not clear, though, who's interested in who.

I think it's actually pretty funny. But Ellen and Rachel are going slightly nuts. Since we never pair off and we're always in a group, it's impossible to get an accurate reading.

I'm feeling pretty confused myself. Jason hasn't made any romantic moves. But we have an understanding. At least I think we do. I wish he would kiss me—a real kiss—so I could know for sure that he was my guy.

SATURDAY, *9:00 P.M.*

Dear Diary,

Jason called late this evening. Guess what? He asked me out. Here's what he said, word for word: "I'd like to take you on a day trip. To someplace special. There aren't a lot of people I could share it with, but I think you would really love it."

We're going to take a private plane. On Tuesday. Three days from now.

When I dropped *that* little tidbit of news at dinner, Jessica Wakefield's stock went up and Lila Fowler's stock went way, way, way down.

SATURDAY, 10:45 P.M.

Dear Diary,

When we went to bed, Marissa came over and sat down. Then she said, in this corny *woman-to-woman* tone—that she didn't begrudge me my relationship with Jason.

She wanted me to know that—in spite of one or two things she might have said—she would never *dream* of coming between us.

(Like I was worried!)

I humored her and told her I appreciated it.

She patted my hand and left me to write in my journal. But now I'm sleepy, so I'm turning off the light.

G'night.

SUNDAY, 4:00 P.M.

Dear Diary,

It's raining, so we're stuck inside with each other and have been all day.

I spent the morning doing what any real Unicorn in my shoes would do—rubbing it in.

Every time Lila mentioned Wiley, I mentioned Jason.

Every time Lila said she missed Wiley, I said I missed Jason.

Every time Lila said Wiley was in high school, I made some remark about how *tall* Jason is.

Finally Lila had had enough. She decided to challenge me.

"You know, Jessica," she said as we were all playing cards after lunch. "Guys aren't like girls."

"You noticed," I said.

Lila gave me this sympathetic smile. "Jessica. That's not what I meant. What I'm trying to tell you is that you might be reading Jason wrong. He might not be as serious about you as you are about him."

Marissa piped up, "Lila's right, Jessica. Guys are like that."

I wanted to grab both of them and knock their heads together. Here was Lila acting like some big relationship expert. And Marissa—who probably knew less than zero about guys—butting in like she knew everything too.

"Now that I'm in a relationship with a guy in high school," Lila started in, "I've had a chance to really see what goes on in a guy's head, and—"

"Don't compare Wiley and Jason," I said angrily, throwing down my discard.

Marissa picked it up, compared it to her other cards, and then smiled happily. (Good thing we weren't playing poker.)

"You're right," Lila said in a snooty voice. "I shouldn't compare them because there really is no comparison. Wiley is in high school, and . . ."

"Game over," I said, folding my cards.

That's when Mandy came in. "Anybody want to take a walk? If I don't get outside, I'm going to lose my mind."

I jumped to my feet. "I'll go." I didn't care that it was raining—I would have gladly headed into a monsoon—as long as I could get away from Lila and Marissa.

Mandy fished her shoes out from under the couch,

and I grabbed a rain slicker out of Pippa's front closet.

Pretty soon we were walking along the road. It was too wet to walk along the beach.

"Lila Fowler is driving me nuts," I said. "How come you're letting her get away with pushing you around?"

Mandy sighed. "I want to stay on her good side so she'll fix me up when we get back. Plus who wants her as an enemy? Don't forget, she's Janet Howell's first cousin. They're not all that different."

I felt a little flicker of fear. Once we got back to Sweet Valley, I wouldn't have Jason. What if Lila got dates for everybody but me? What if everybody except me had this great social life? What if Lila decided to ruin me? She could do it.

The rain had slacked off to a drizzle. I looked at the beautiful purple mountaintops and the misty sky and felt totally dismal.

"Jessica," Mandy said. "If we do wind up at different schools next year, we'll still be friends, right?"

I looked at Mandy. Was she sincere? Or was she just trying to hedge her bets, trying to be Lila's friend *and* mine? "Of course," I said, wondering if it was really true. I didn't think it was. I was mad at Mandy in a way I couldn't really explain. She was going against everything that she believed—just to stay on Lila's good side.

On some level I just couldn't respect her anymore.

Before I had time to think about it, we were at the end of the beach and there was the Surf Shack. I realized that's where Mandy had been heading all along. "Want to go in?" she asked.

I started to say something snotty like—*Did you get a permission slip from Lila?*—but I stopped myself in time.

We stepped inside. Carl was sitting behind the counter, reading a magazine.

When he looked up, he gave both of us a big grin—but something incredible happened. He looked right at *me* and smiled. An intimate kind of smile. Like there was something between us. "Hi!" He sounded really glad to see me. "I was just thinking about you."

Talk about ironic! Finally Mandy gets up the nerve to talk to Carl, but Carl's more interested in talking to . . . me.

I hate to say this—but it made me feel *great!*

I remembered what Lila had said on the beach. *"If you don't stop acting like Marissa's big sister and best buddy, the Unicorns are going to go one way and you're going to go another."*

Well, I thought suddenly, *maybe it's time.*

Maybe we've all outgrown one another.

I loved my old friends. But my old friends didn't really seem like my friends anymore. And I was sick of the whole "Lilapalooza."

I realized something—I didn't care anymore. Suddenly confidence was pulsing through my veins. Who cared about Lila? About Janet? About Peter Feldman? About Wiley Upjohn?

And who cared about the Unicorns?

Not me anymore.

If Lila didn't get me dates, I'd get my own.

If my old friends ditched me, I'd make new ones.

In spite of the rain outside, in spite of the dark clouds overheard, in spite of the fact that Jason hadn't really kissed me, I suddenly felt great. I wasn't afraid anymore.

Eleven

◇

Dear Diary,

Life has never looked better.

Kimberly and Marissa left early this morning with Pippa to go to the new Maui gift shop.

Ellen and Rachel went to the mall.

So it was just me, Mandy, and Lila in the apartment when Carl called. For me.

He said it was his day off, and did I want another surfing lesson? Then he said I had natural talent, and it would be a shame not to develop it. I told Carl I'd meet him in half an hour, then I hung up and started gloating.

I turned to Lila. "Can I borrow your waterproof eye shadow?"

She raised her eyebrows. "What for?"

"Carl just invited me surfing."

Mandy's mouth fell open. She stared at me like I was the biggest traitor in the whole world. I pretended not to notice. Lila looked like she didn't know what to say. "But what about Jason?" she asked.

"What about him?" I asked in this innocent voice.

"Y-Y-You said you guys had something going," she sputtered.

"And you told me it was all in my head," I countered in this fake gullible tone.

Lila threw down her magazine and left the room in a huff. Mandy gave me a hurt look, then followed Lila.

I went into the room I was sharing with Kimberly and Marissa and started to get ready. I washed and dried my hair even though I knew I'd be going into the ocean. And I gave myself a full makeup job with all the waterproof stuff I could find.

Lila came in. "If I did this to Wiley, he'd break up with me."

"Did what?" I asked.

"Cheated on him."

I rolled my eyes. "Get a grip, Lila. You're not engaged to Wiley. You can surf with somebody, can't you?"

She pressed her lips together, trying to think up a comeback. I had her right where I wanted her.

I gave her a real patronizing smile. "Look at it this way," I told her. "It'll be good practice for next year."

She frowned. "What are you talking about?"

I opened my eyes wide. "Next year I have no intention of letting one guy take up all my time. So this is a great way to learn how to juggle more than one boy."

Lila's eyes narrowed. "Jessica Wakefield, you are really pushing your luck."

"At least I've got luck to push," I quipped. "I don't see anybody else trying to juggle two guys."

And with that, I grabbed my tote bag and strutted out of the apartment.

I met Carl down by the water, and we had a great time. In spite of acting like hot stuff in front of Lila, I was worried that I would feel shy and awkward with him. Carl looks sixteen. I wondered if he knew how old I was. People always say I look older.

But once I got to the beach, I didn't feel awkward at all. In fact, it was more like being with Steven than being with a boyfriend. Carl didn't act like a guy with a crush or anything. He seemed serious about teaching me to surf. Too serious! Long after I got pooped, he was still making me paddle out and try to stand up. I did manage to ride one wave all the way in on my knees. But I never could stand up.

After that, Carl asked if I wanted to get something to drink, and we walked down to the teen club. He got us a couple of sodas, and we sat outside on the deck.

"So tell me about life in California," he said.

I told him life in California was pretty great. Turns out Carl is a native of Hawaii. He lives here all year, and his family has been here for as long as anybody can remember. He's part Chinese and part Pacific Islander.

Also, it turned out he's not sixteen. He's fifteen

but very tall for his age. We talked and laughed and goofed, and then he walked me back to the condo.

He didn't try to kiss me or anything. I was glad. Because really and truly, I wouldn't want to hurt Mandy. Besides, my heart belonged to Jason. But I couldn't help feeling totally cocky when I got back upstairs.

Here's the score.

> Mandy—0
> Kimberly—1
> Rachel—0
> Ellen—0
> Lila—1
> Jessica—2

Numbers don't lie.

I rule.

MONDAY, 10:00 P.M.

Dear Diary,

Here's an excerpt from tonight's conversation about tomorrow's *"big date"*:

"So Jason won't tell you anything at all about where you're going?" Ellen asked me.

I shook my head. "Nope. It's a surprise." I gave my hair a last shot of spray.

"And it's on a different island? Which island?" Ellen pressed.

"Does it matter?" Marissa gasped. "It's another island. They're going away together. It's the most romantic thing that's ever happened to any of us."

I heard Lila let out this little squeak of irritation.

"Watch that 'us' stuff," she warned Marissa. "You're not a Unicorn yet."

But Marissa was unsquelchable. "OK, then. It's the most romantic thing that's ever happened to any of *you* guys. I won't even include myself because for all you know, I've had dozens and dozens of romantic adventures."

"Stifle yourself," Kimberly told her.

Marissa just giggled.

Everybody was in our room, watching me get ready for my big day of total romance, which starts tomorrow morning.

I'm doing my hair tonight because Jason is picking me up at 7 A.M.

Lila is eating her heart out. She even tried to get my date canceled by telling Pippa about it.

I guess she thought Pippa would forbid me to go. Instead Pippa waited until everybody but me was out of the condo to ask me if I would mind her calling Jason's family and touching base.

I said it was OK. (Did I have a choice?) Pippa phoned Jason's dad. I guess Mr. Landry got the Pippa Haver household seal of approval. After they spoke, Pippa said it was cool for me to go and never even mentioned to anybody that she had checked up on everything.

In a way, it was even cooler that things turned out like that. As far as Lila knew, I was making all my own decisions just like a real grown-up while *she* still has to ask permission to go to a movie with Wiley.

Am I riding high or what?

Twelve

Dear Diary,

I should never have written that "Am I riding high" line. It's right up there with . . . *"All our problems were over."*

As planned, Jason and his dad picked me up at 7 A.M. Mr. Landry drove us to the little airport where Pippa keeps her plane.

Jason's dad took us inside, and there was our old friend, Mr. Hajit. He and Jason joked around a bit—it was pretty clear they knew each other well. Mr. Hajit told Jason's dad he would bring us back around 6 P.M.

Mr. Landry said he'd be back to pick us up this evening and told us to have fun.

Mr. Hajit told us we were the only passengers on this run, so we might as well get started.

The flight only took about fifteen minutes. The little island we landed on had just a tiny airstrip. No airport—no building at all! Mr. Hajit told us to be back around 5:30 and opened the door. We hopped out, and Mr. Hajit taxied to the end of the airstrip and took off again, soaring away over our heads.

As the noise of the engine died away I began to hear the sounds of the island. The birds, the wind, and the surf.

Suddenly there were only two people in the whole world. Me and Jason, alone on an island paradise.

I felt nervous but excited. What would we do next? Go explore some romantic forest? Climb to the top of a volcano? Swim in some incredibly romantic cove?

That's when the Jeep pulled up.

And guess who was sitting in the front seat next to the driver, wearing a cap that said Camp Aloha and a big grin?

Hal, the sand rat.

I wanted to groan.

Jason turned to me and put his arm around my shoulders. "I wanted you to see Camp Aloha," he said. "It's Bring a Special Friend Day. All the counselors are supposed to bring someone who might be interested in volunteering. You're so patient and caring—I knew you'd love it."

My heart sank right down into my shoes.

This was my big surprise!!!

No *way* did I want to spend the day at some stupid summer camp for obnoxious kids.

The Jeep came to a stop. I spotted Rafe and Larry,

sitting in the back with a couple of little boys and girls. I noticed that one of them had on leg braces.

"Hi, Jessica!" Rafe and Larry smiled and waved like they were really glad to see me. "We think it's great you came," Rafe said.

"We came yesterday to help out," Larry added.

What could I do except smile and say how thrilled I was to be there? I had to act gracious. But it was a major effort not to burst into disappointed tears.

Jason helped me into the Jeep and climbed in himself. Hal stared hard at me. "I know you. You're the girl with the spinach mouth. Show everybody your green teeth."

I wanted to smack him. Instead I smiled, showing him my pearly whites. His face fell. "What happened?" he asked in a disappointed tone. Obviously he thought a girl with green teeth was much better than a girl with regular teeth.

"It wore off," I said.

"Can you make them green again?" he asked. He looked at me hopefully.

"Nope," I said. "Sorry."

Hal wasn't thrilled with that answer, but he seemed to accept it.

I was so bummed out that I hardly noticed the scenery as we drove to the camp. I'm sure under more *romantic* circumstances I would have come back with a lot of very poetic descriptions.

But I wasn't there on a date. Basically I was there to baby-sit.

When we pulled into the camp, I saw a lot of

people around my own age. I recognized a few
kids from the beach. Some of them recognized me
and came over to say hello.

One guy said that Jason must think a lot of me
or else he wouldn't have invited me here. That
made me feel a little bit better.

Jason took my hand (which made me feel a *lot*
better) and said he wanted to show me around.

"Most of these kids are recovering from cancer,"
he said in a soft voice. "Last summer I suggested
that we start trying to get kids like Hal—kids with
emotional problems—involved. I think it makes
them feel better about themselves. I know helping
other people makes *me* feel better about myself.
And you're just like I am. I can tell."

I felt my cheeks flush because I knew the truth. I
wasn't like Jason at all. His image of me was all
wrong, and I felt ashamed. Let's face it, I spend
most of my time thinking about myself. I wish that
weren't true—but . . .

Oh, well . . . let's not go there. I feel rotten enough.

Back to the story.

Jason showed me the cabins and the physical
therapy center. He showed me where the kids who
were still getting chemo had their own cabin attached to a medical building.

Then it was time for activities.

Jason, Rafe, Larry, and I were supposed to help
a group of kids make puppets and put on a show
for the other kids.

I was not thrilled. *But* . . . I do know a thing or

two about entertaining kids. (The Unicorns did a lot of volunteer work at a day care center last year.)

The group of kids we were assigned to work with were actually pretty cute. (Hal was not one of them—thank goodness!) There were four little boys and three little girls.

Rafe suggested that we put on a show about Martian invaders.

The little boys all thought that was a great idea.

The little girls weren't thrilled.

Jason suggested a fairy tale. Something everyone knew already, like *Cinderella.*

The girls smiled and the boys groaned.

I suggested a compromise. *Cinderella in Outer Space.* That got everybody excited.

Step one was making puppets. We used empty coconut halves for heads and all kinds of seashells, plants, and bark to make ugly Martian stepsisters.

Our fairy godmother had mother-of-pearl eyes, gorgeous ferns for hair, and a palm frond for a wand. The stepmother was a big octopus. We made an octopus head out of a sack of sand. It flopped around in a very realistic way.

Cinderella was a bromeliad—which is a huge pink exotic flower. She went to a ball on the planet Jupiter, where she fell in love with the prince, who was a big conch shell.

Hey! I know it doesn't make sense, but it was set in outer space, so anything went.

The horrible stepmother (from planet Day-Old Fish Sticks) was hoping to take over the planet

Earth so her ugly daughters (giant sea monsters) could eat all the earthlings.

It was pretty hilarious. The more outrageous our story got, the more creative the guys became. And the more creative the guys became, the more fun the kids had.

By the time we put on the show, our story had almost nothing to do with Cinderella. Nobody cared. They roared with laughter and thought the puppets were great.

I actually had so much fun, I forgot how angry and disappointed I had felt when we arrived.

At lunch we all sat at long picnic tables and had fruit salad and peanut butter sandwiches. Some of the kids needed help eating, and Rafe and Larry seemed very cool helping out with that.

Hal wanted to sit on Jason's lap during lunch. I sat by Jason—so that meant I had to make conversation with Hal.

First thing out of his mouth: "Do you have a boyfriend?"

Jason blushed, and so did I. Fortunately some other kid tried to take Hal's cookie, and that gave him something to think about besides me and my love life.

Did I *have* a love life? I wondered.

I looked at Jason.

He was mopping up soda where Hal had spilled it, but his cheeks were flaming.

During the afternoon we took some kids on a nature hike. We used trails that Jason had marked last summer.

When it was finally time to leave, there were a lot of people going back. Not just me and Jason but other visitors who had come from other islands.

We didn't even get to sit together on the plane. Jason's dad was waiting for us at the little airport. When they dropped me back at the condo, Jason gave me a good-bye kiss on the cheek. I wondered if he would have kissed me for real if his dad hadn't been sitting in the car.

The truth was—I had no idea. I had everybody else convinced that Jason was my boyfriend. How could I convince *him*?

Jason said he and his dad were going to a family thing tomorrow and then he had to go back to camp tomorrow night. But he would see me the following weekend.

Then—*poof*—he was gone.

TUESDAY, 10:40 P.M.

Dear Diary,

I know it's wrong to lie, but I'm not sure that what I'm doing is actually lying.

When I got up to the apartment, I'd already decided how I would handle the Unicorns. I would just refuse to answer questions. Anything anybody asked me—I'd just smile like I knew something they didn't.

So that's what I did.

"What island did you go to?" Kimberly asked.

I told them, and they all ran to Pippa's maps to look it up. "Wow! It's really small," Mandy commented.

"But big enough to get lost on, I bet," Marissa said with a giggle. "Was it gorgeous?"

I smiled.

"Did you guys take a walk?" Rachel wanted to know.

I smiled.

"Did he kiss you?" Ellen blurted out—asking the question that I knew everybody was dying to ask.

"Ellen!" I exclaimed. I just smiled again—like I *really* knew something they didn't. Then I said I was going to take a bath. I acted like I was embarrassed that they were asking me so many personal questions.

I went into the bathroom, ran a hot tub, and sank down in it to think.

All in all, I'd had a fun day. But it sure wasn't the romantic getaway day I'd envisioned.

Then I had a horrible fear. Maybe Jason thought I was gross. Or maybe he thought I was a big nerd for hanging with Marissa. A nice nerd who would enjoy volunteering. Too nerdy to be crushworthy. Not anybody he'd want to date.

The thought was so horrible and scary, I sank down into the water and wished I were a fish so I could stay down there and never have to come up and face him again.

When my lungs felt like they might burst, I came up for air.

What was I going to do? The only way that I could keep Lila in check was through this boyfriend thing. Without Jason, I had nothing.

Then I remembered Carl.

So, Dear Diary, Jessica's plan for image recovery is to make a big play for Carl tomorrow.

Wish me luck.

WEDNESDAY, 1:10 P.M.

Dear Diary,

This morning I got all dolled up and ready to work my charms on Carl. We all lay out on our towels after breakfast as usual.

For once I was really grateful that Marissa was there. She was tooting my horn so loud, I didn't have to.

"I wish you had taken a camera with you," she said. "I keep picturing you and Jason together—standing on a high cliff, looking out over a waterfall. Was it like that? Was it?"

I did my smile thing, and she flopped over on her back and groaned. "Oh, I'm sooo jealous. Jason is so adorable. So nice. So . . . everything a girl could want."

"Jason isn't all that," Lila snapped—really peeved that everybody was more interested in my romance than in hers.

I swung into action. "I think I'll walk down to the Surf Shack and see Carl," I said, trying to sound casual.

I stood up, pulled some shorts on over my suit, and started down the beach. I could hear them whispering about me as I walked away.

Down at the end of the beach I saw Carl out waxing the boards. He smiled and waved. "Hey! I'm working today, but you can keep me company."

I sat down on the bench and dug my toes down

into the sand. "I'll be officially off duty in an hour," he told me. "Want to surf in a little while?"

"You mean *try* to surf?"

He chuckled. "All it takes is practice. You'll get it. You've got the gift."

"I'll bet you say that to all the girls."

"I do," he admitted. "To all the guys too. Anybody who really wants to surf can surf. All you need is confidence."

He went inside to answer the telephone, and I watched the gulls circling over the ocean.

Confidence was all anybody needed to do anything—if you believed what magazines told you. But this whole trip has been like a confidence seesaw.

One day I'm confident. The next day I'm terrified.

Carl came out of the Surf Shack with a piece of paper. "Hey! That was some guy trying to get in touch with Marissa. He tried to call Pippa, but she's got an unlisted number. He said he saw her surfing with me, so he called here."

I took the piece of paper, and my eyes almost fell out of my head.

Message for Marissa
Call Peter Feldman

WEDNESDAY, 5:00 P.M.

Dear Diary,

After Carl gave me the message, he and I went out and goofed around in the surf. I rode in on my knees again. I still can't stand up, but Carl says it's only a matter of time.

Again he didn't really act romantic. I think he doesn't have a crush on me after all. He just likes me as a friend.

Is *anybody* ever going to like me as a *"girlfriend"*?

Mandy's still under the impression that Carl and I have a thing going. She's been giving me the cold shoulder all afternoon. Do I care?

I thought I didn't, but now I'm not sure.

I keep "forgetting" to give Marissa the message from Peter. It's horrible, but now I'm just as worried as Lila about what Peter might think. Marissa seems to think I'm her very best friend in the whole world. If Peter asks her out—(a) he'll find out she's a seventh-grader, (b) he'll realize within ten minutes that she's a motormouth nerd and not a cool surfer chick, and (c) she'll tell him that she considers Jessica Wakefield her very best pal.

By the time I get back to Sweet Valley, I'll be at the top of the dork list and nobody in the *eighth* grade even will ask me out—never mind guys in high school.

So that piece of paper is still in the pocket of my shorts.

I feel guilty. But I'm so used to feeling guilty, it doesn't faze me that much anymore.

WEDNESDAY, 7:00 P.M.

Dear Diary,

Today Lila comes in after taking a walk and says, "Jessica, I want to see you in my room."

Just like that. Like she's the school principal or something.

I started to tell her to jump off the balcony, but something about her face scared me. She looked really mean. And really serious.

As a compromise, I went to her room, but I took my time, yawning and stopping to get a soda first.

When I went in, she told me to close the door—she had something private to tell me.

Let me tell you, she was really starting to work my nerves. Still, I closed the door.

"I was out on the beach, and I had a very interesting talk with Rafe and Larry."

My heart sank. Uh-oh.

Lila smiled. "They told me all about your fabulous romantic date."

Uh-oh.

"They told me how it was just you and Jason, and a hundred other camp counselors, and little kids."

I sat down on the end of Rachel's bed and didn't say anything.

Lila crossed her arms. "I think you owe me an apology. For lying. And for actually comparing your pathetic little friendship to my relationship with Wiley."

I took a sip of my soda. "Forget it."

"No way. If you don't apologize, I'm going to make your life miserable. I'll tell the others. And furthermore, I'll tell everybody when we get back home."

I put my hand down into my pocket and pulled out the little piece of paper. "I don't think so," I said, staring at Lila through narrowed eyes.

"What do you mean?"

"I mean if you don't back off, I will give Marissa the message that Peter Feldman called her and wants her to call him back."

The color drained from Lila's face. "That's a lie."

"No lie. If you don't believe me, ask Carl. But that probably isn't a good idea. Because Carl might mention it to Marissa and . . ." I shrugged. "Well, we all know how thrilled Marissa is to be considered for Unicorn membership. She'd probably love calling Peter to tell him about it."

"This is total blackmail," Lila sputtered.

"What did you think it was when you were threatening me?" I shot back. "How come there's one set of rules for Lila and another set of rules for everybody else? If you mess with me, I'll make sure that Marissa and Peter Feldman have the dream date of the summer." I stormed out and slammed the door behind me. Then I went into my room, feeling sick and ashamed and angry.

I don't understand what is happening. Somewhere along the line Lila has gone from being my best friend to being my archenemy.

WEDNESDAY, 10:00 P.M.

Dear Diary,

I keep waiting for Lila to make a move, but she hasn't. Nobody is acting strange, so I don't think she's told anybody. But I'm *watching my back!*

THURSDAY, 3:40 P.M.

Dear Diary,

Today I went down to the Surf Shack to see Carl. He asked me if I remembered to give Marissa the message. I told him that I had, but Marissa wasn't interested in Peter and was embarrassed about the attention. I made Carl promise not to say anything to Marissa about it.

Am I good or what?

THURSDAY, 6:50 P.M.

Dear Diary,

Later Carl came down to where we were hanging on the beach. Mandy clammed up and wouldn't talk at all.

Carl was friendly to everybody. He and I went for a walk, and he told me he was going to be working the bar at the teen club tonight and said we should all plan on going.

I thought about it, but I realized if we went, Peter Feldman might be there. He might see Marissa and go talk to her, and the whole ugly truth would come out.

So I said we had other plans.

I am getting *so* sneaky.

FRIDAY, 10:00 A.M.

Dear Diary,

Jason called. He got back today and will be here for the weekend. He asked me to go to the teen club. It's a date. A real date. I'm so glad I didn't tell the others it's teen night. Now I'll be the only one to go. Take *that*, Lila Fowler. Ha-ha-ha-ha!

FRIDAY, 1:00 P.M.

Dear Diary,

Foiled! Kimberly found out it was teen night at the club. Now they're all planning to go as a big girl group. What am I going to do?

FRIDAY, 5:00 P.M.

Dear Diary,

I have such good luck: Marissa's got an earache! Pippa took her to the doctor this afternoon. The doctor put her on antibiotics and told Pippa she should stay in bed for a few days. Yay!

Kimberly went with Pippa and Marissa to the doctor. When they got back, Pippa called Marissa's mom and stayed on the phone with her for a long time.

Mandy and I were in the living room with Kimberly. We could hear Pippa's voice through the wall. It sounded like Pippa was doing an awful lot of reassuring.

"Wow," Mandy said. "Marissa's mom must really be worried."

Kimberly stretched out on the sofa. "Marissa's mom is real protective. Marissa's got some heavy-duty food allergies, and her mom is always worried that she might accidentally eat something she shouldn't."

"What's she allergic to?" Mandy asked curiously.

"Mainly she's allergic to peanuts—which doesn't sound like a big deal until you start thinking of all the stuff that has peanut oil in it."

"Jessica," Pippa said, coming into the room. "Marissa would like to see you."

I got up and went into the bedroom. Marissa was lying there, looking miserable.

"Does it hurt much?" I asked.

She shook her head. "No. I'm just bummed because I want to go with you guys tonight."

"We'll miss you," I lied.

She smiled at me. "Thanks, Jessica."

"I'll get out and let you sleep. Kimberly and I will use the hall bathroom so we don't wake you up."

"No," she said. "Get dressed in here. Even if I can't go, I'll at least get to listen to you guys talk while you get ready. It's not as good as going myself, but it makes it easier knowing somebody will be out having fun even if I can't."

Sometimes Marissa really surprises me. If I had been sick, I wouldn't have wanted anybody to have fun if I couldn't go along.

Then she blinked at me. "My birthday is coming up."

"Really?"

She nodded into her pillow.

"Know what I want?"

"What?"

"To be a full-fledged Unicorn," she murmured. Then she closed her eyes and drifted off to sleep.

Thirteen

Dear Diary,
    What a night!
    I'm sleeping in the living room with Mandy and Ellen. Kimberly is sleeping with Pippa. Pippa said Marissa is running a fever and needs her rest—Marissa has a room to herself. That's why we're not sleeping in our regular beds.
    First of all, let me write down what I learned tonight so I don't forget it.
    Guys like girls who are enthusiastic!
    I really need to remember that. Because Lila's got it all wrong.
    Anyway—where was I? Oh, yeah. Jason picked me up, and we walked together to the teen club. When he found out Marissa wasn't going, he was very bummed and made me promise to

tell her hello from him when I got home.

When we got to the club, we went to the bar, and Carl was doing his blender-drink thing. Rafe and Larry were there, and they had on matching purple polo shirts with the camp logo on them. They asked me if everybody would be coming. And they looked happy when I said they were. And that Rachel and Ellen were looking forward to seeing them. (Hey! It couldn't hurt.)

Larry and Rafe grinned, then exchanged a quizzical look and a shrug. I put my hand over my mouth to hide my smile. It was pretty clear that Ellen and Rachel weren't the only ones who were confused about who was interested in who.

I decided the four of them were in for an interesting evening.

Carl made all the guys purple drinks to go with their shirts. He made me a bright pink drink to go with my sundress and matching sandals. I looked great even if I do say so myself.

Jason said he was going to talk to the DJ and make some requests. He went inside with Rafe and Larry. I stayed near the bar so I could watch Carl until they came back. He asked me where Marissa was, and I told him she was sick.

Carl said it was too bad that she wouldn't be coming. Then he told me that Peter Feldman had come by and asked about her.

"Hey," I joked. "I'm starting to get jealous. Why is everyone so eager to see Marissa?"

Carl grinned. "Seriously?"

"Sure," I answered, curious about what he was going to say.

"Marissa's a cute girl," he said, cutting up chunks of pineapple for a drink. "But mainly she's the kind of person who makes you feel good about yourself. She doesn't seem like she's making judgments all the time. She's just . . . I don't know . . . friendly. That's probably the biggest beauty secret in the whole world."

A whole bunch of people came up to ask for drinks, so I wandered into the club to find Jason. On the way in, Peter Feldman came over to me and asked where Marissa was. I told him she was sick, and he said he was sorry to hear it.

The other Unicorns got to the club about half an hour after Jason and I did. It was a little weird at first. But then Rafe and Larry asked Ellen and Rachel to dance. Peter Feldman asked Lila. And two other guys challenged Kimberly and Mandy to a game of darts.

Once everybody had somebody to dance with, flirt with, or hang with, it was almost like the last time we came to the teen club. We were a tight group again. Friends. All for one and one for all.

How long would it last? I wondered.

Saturday, 10:00 a.m.

Dear Diary,

Marissa is feeling a lot better. Her birthday is Tuesday. Pippa said she would take us all out to dinner at a fancy restaurant to celebrate. It would have to wait until Thursday, though, because she's busy trying to get the gift shop ready for the opening. She's spending all day, every day, at wholesale gift shows.

She's so busy, she sent Kimberly to Maui for a few days to help out. Kimberly's going to stay with Steve and his folks. Lucky Kimberly!

Since we knew we had a fancy dinner coming up, we decided to hit the mall. Rachel, Ellen, Mandy, Lila, and I all headed over on the bus. Marissa didn't want to go. She was still tired from being sick.

It was at the mall that Lila made her move.

We were all sitting in a café, eating avocado, pineapple, and mango salads when she got this cat-that-swallowed-the-canary look on her face.

"Peter Feldman is going back to Sweet Valley today. He's probably on the plane right now," she said.

"Oh?"

"And since Marissa's birthday is coming up, I think we should give Marissa a surprise party," she said.

"Really?" I wondered what the catch was.

"I think we should surprise Marissa by inviting all the guys she knows to the party—and making sure she eats enough peanuts to cover her with splotches from head to toe."

I lifted my spoon. "Wait a minute!"

Lila raised her eyebrow. "Do you have a problem with this?"

"Yes," I protested. "That's a horrible thing to do. We

don't know what happens when Marissa eats peanuts."

"My cousin has an allergy to peanuts," Ellen said. "Whenever she eats them, she gets hives."

"Yeah, but that doesn't mean Marissa will get hives. She could have a serious reaction." I looked around the table. Every face looked stony. None of my "friends" were rallying to my side here. Not even Mandy, who is usually the first to vote "nay" on stuff like this.

Maybe she was so angry with me about Carl, she couldn't think straight. I cleared my throat and tried to sound as reasonable as possible. "If we do something that mean, Pippa will probably send us all home."

Mandy shrugged. "So?"

Wow! Mandy really was furious!

Rachel leaned forward. "We've only got another week. What's the big deal if we wind up going home early? Lila says Wiley's friends all need dates starting this week anyway."

Lila nodded. "There are picnics and parties and even a dance at Janet's house. Don't you get it, Jessica? We're just wasting our time here."

I sat back. *Were* we wasting our time? This was our last summer together, but it wasn't making us closer. It was driving us apart.

Lila leaned over and whispered in my ear, "Peter Feldman is gone. That means you've got squat on me. But Jason is still here, and I could tell everybody the truth about your 'romantic day.' I could also tell *Jason* how disappointed you were."

"You wouldn't," I growled.

"Oh, yes, I would," she whispered. Then she sat back and calmly finished eating her salad. "The party is on. Day after tomorrow."

"Ellen can take Marissa shopping or something while we get everything ready," Rachel said.

Lila took a little pad out of her purse and started making a list. "Things to buy. One. Peanuts. Two. Peanut butter. Three. Peanut oil."

I realized then that I am the biggest coward in the world. I knew I was going to go along with it. Because when we all got back to Sweet Valley, Lila was going to be calling the shots. And I needed to be on her good side.

I really hate myself.

I hate myself almost as much as I hate Lila Fowler.

SUNDAY, 10:40 A.M.

Dear Diary,

Jason called, and Lila picked up the phone. She invited him and Rafe and Larry to the surprise birthday party for Marissa.

He said they'd be there. When I got on the phone, he said he was really looking forward to the party and asked me if I wanted to go help out at the camp tomorrow. I could spend the night there, and we could come back together the next morning.

I said yes. I didn't really want to go help out at the camp, but I didn't want to be here either.

When I hung up the phone, I realized that I was going to have to explain where I was going. "Jason invited me to a party at the camp where he works.

I'm going to spend tomorrow night there. We'll come back together Tuesday morning."

"A camp?" Ellen said, wrinkling up her nose. "That doesn't sound very romantic."

"This isn't that kind of date," I huffed.

"Unlike your *other* date with Jason," put in evil Lila.

I shut up. I really don't need Lila making me feel any worse than I already do.

SUNDAY, 11:11 A.M.

Dear Diary,

Marissa is up and around. Talking a mile a minute and minding everybody's business.

I hate to say this—but things were a lot nicer when she was sick. We didn't have her tagging along and acting like a big know-it-all. I feel horrible knowing what the other girls are planning. On the other hand, I'm glad I'm going away tomorrow because it'll give me a break from Marissa.

Ellen is telling everybody to get their stuff together so we can hit the beach.

More later.

SUNDAY, 7:00 P.M.

Dear Diary,

We were hanging down at the beach when Carl came over with five surfboards on his head. He invited everybody to take one and give it a try.

Of course, Marissa grabbed one and ran out into the waves without looking back. I took one, Rachel took one, and Ellen took one.

"So, Mandy," Carl said. "Want to come out?"

Mandy didn't even smile. She just examined the end of her extension. I could see that her face was flushed and she was nervous. "No, thanks," she said in a flat voice. "Surfing isn't my thing."

"Mine either," Lila volunteered.

Both of them sounded completely disinterested.

Carl and I walked out into the water together. "Am I making a pest of myself?" he asked me.

I laughed. "No way. Why do you ask?"

He shrugged. "I don't know. Lila and Mandy looked like they wanted to get rid of me. I thought maybe I was intruding."

I shook my head. "No. They're afraid of looking stupid."

"I can relate," he said with a grin. "But anybody who sits on a beach when they can be out on a board looks stupid to me."

With that, he jumped on his board and paddled out. "Come on!" he shouted.

I got up on my board and paddled after him. Pretty soon we were all bobbing on the waves—me, Carl, Rachel, Marissa, and Ellen.

We felt the ocean swell. A big one was coming. A really big one.

"Get ready," Carl said, turning his board so that it pointed toward the beach.

We staggered ourselves so we wouldn't collide.

The swell picked us up, lifting us higher and higher.

"*Go!*" Carl shouted.

All of us started paddling in, trying to catch the wave.

To my right, I saw Ellen try to climb up. It was too soon. There wasn't enough momentum. She fell off the board before she had even managed to get to her knees.

Rachel was on one knee and trying to stand.

Bam! She wiped out.

Suddenly the wave grabbed me and the board. We were hurtling toward the beach. The thrust steadied the board underneath me.

I got up on my knees. The board didn't even teeter.

I got up on my feet—in a crouch.

The board was still steady underneath me and moving forward in a smooth path.

I stood up.

I'm not kidding.

I actually stood up! *I was surfing!*

I had my arms out for balance, but after a few seconds I felt so at ease I let them hang loosely at my sides. It was like skateboarding, only better.

When I looked over and saw Marissa and Carl surfing side by side, I felt like we were sharing something incredibly special.

Finally the wave played out. We were almost to the shore. I jumped off my board, and so did Carl and Marissa. Carl grabbed me and twirled me around. Marissa jumped up and down, screaming like a maniac. "You did it!" she yelled. "You did it! You did it!"

I looked over to see if Lila and Mandy had been watching my big moment. Both of them were staring at their books, paying no attention whatsoever.

Carl's face fell. After all, this wasn't just a big moment for me; it was a big moment for him. He was a surfing instructor—and I was living proof that he was a good one.

"I guess they're right," he said in this disappointed tone. "Surfing really isn't their thing."

Rachel and Ellen came paddling in on their boards. "Nice going," Rachel said to me.

Ellen gave me a high five.

"Come on," Carl told everybody. "Let's try it again."

We all went back out and spent the next two hours having a ball. I managed to get up four times. Marissa got up so many times, I lost count. Ellen rode in twice on her knees. Ditto Rachel.

By the time we came out of the water, Lila and Mandy had already gone up to the condo. Carl collected the boards. "I'll see you guys tomorrow?"

"Not Jessica," Marissa told him. "She's going to help Jason at that camp."

Carl looked disappointed. "Too bad. But I'll see you at the—"

He caught himself just in time. I knew he'd been about to say "at the party." Marissa's surprise party.

Marissa didn't notice. She was too busy telling Kimberly how the Haver women were born to surf. Carl winked at me and made a funny "that-was-close" face. He stepped nearer to me and lowered his voice. "You'll be back in time for the party, right?"

I nodded. "Definitely."

He smiled. "OK, then. See you there."

He walked off with the boards balanced on his

head. I watched him go and had another incredible insight. Life is a lot like surfing.

It looks easy.

But it's not.

MONDAY, *8:00* A.M.

Dear Diary,

I'm sitting out front waiting for Jason to pick me up. I'm actually looking forward to going back to the camp. I've got some ideas for new puppet shows.

Here comes Jason with his dad. Gag! Hal is with them.

MONDAY, *11:40* P.M.

Dear Diary,

I can't sleep. I've got a *real* problem.

Mr. Hajit flew us to the island this morning, and the camp director picked us up in his Jeep. When we got to the camp, they were having a field day. Only instead of stuff like relay races, the competitions were all silly things. Things like—who could keep a straight face the longest when Jason was doing his chimpanzee imitation.

Good thing I wasn't competing. I couldn't keep a straight face for six seconds. Who knew Jason was such a comedian?

After that, we all took another nature hike and competed to see who could name the most flora and fauna. I was way out of my league there—so I just kept an eye on the stragglers and made sure we didn't lose anybody.

Before I knew it, it was time for dinner. We

cooked hot dogs over a fire. Jason cooked mine for
me and asked me what I liked on it. He brought me
a plate and a soda and was really polite about making sure I had everything I wanted.

In a funny way, this felt more like a date than
anything we had done so far. I ate my hot dog, but
I didn't have much appetite.

I couldn't stop thinking about what was going on
back at the condo. Maybe Marissa would see all the
peanut stuff they had bought. Maybe Mandy would
break down and call Kimberly and Kimberly would
put a stop to it. Maybe . . .

Jason noticed that I hadn't eaten much. He
asked if I felt OK. I told him I felt fine, I just wasn't
very hungry.

Somebody got out a guitar, and we all sang
along. Jason sat next to me and put his arm around
me. But I couldn't relax. I felt stiff and self-conscious.
I know he sensed it, and he took his arm away.

After the kids all went to bed, the counselors sat
around talking for a while. They seemed like a nice
group of people. Really nice.

When the fire died out, it was time to go to bed.
Jason introduced me to a girl named Natasha and
told me I would be sharing a tent with her. When
he told me good night, he squeezed my hand, but
he didn't kiss me.

There *were* a lot of people standing around. It
wouldn't have been totally appropriate. But I really
wanted to know what was going on. Did he want
to be my friend? Or my boyfriend?

Natasha and I walked up the path to her tent. I noticed she was eating a cheese sandwich. "Didn't you get enough dinner?" I joked.

She smiled. "I'm allergic to hot dogs," she said. "Something in the preservatives. I can't eat any cold cuts or stuff like that."

Suddenly I felt light-headed. "What happens?" I asked. "Do you break out in hives?"

She shook her head. "I *wish*. No. I have a really horrible reaction. My throat swells up, and I can't breathe. Twice I've had to go to the emergency room and get injections of Adrenalin. I was lucky to be near a hospital. I could have died."

When she said that, my feet went numb and my hands felt icy cold. Could Marissa have a violent reaction like that?

I've been trying to sleep for almost two hours. But I can't. I'm too anxious. I have to get back first thing in the morning and stop Lila.

Fourteen

◇

Dear Diary,

It's almost 2:30. Lila and the others are setting up the peanut-laced refreshments. I can't stand the suspense. Pretty soon the party is going to start and there's not going to be any birthday girl.

I don't know what's going to happen. All I know is that Marissa won't be eating any peanuts.

I guess I did finally fall asleep last night, but I jerked awake as soon as the sun was up. I pulled on my clothes, grabbed my duffel bag, and hurried to the main lodge.

Jason was there, helping set up for breakfast.

"Jason, I have to go back," I told him.

"We're going back on the eleven A.M. flight," he said.

"I can't wait—this is an emergency. Can you take

me down to the airstrip? I have to be on the first plane back."

Jason took me aside. "What's the matter? What's wrong? Did something happen?"

I shook my head. "I can't explain. I just have to go back."

He looked hurt. "Does it have anything to do with me?"

"No!" My voice broke. "But I have to go back. I have to go back now." I was close to panicking, and I guess he heard it in my voice.

"OK," he said quietly. "I'll get somebody to take us."

I don't know what Jason told the camp director, but he didn't try to argue with us and we were at the airstrip when Mr. Hajit landed for the first relay.

Half an hour later Mr. Landry was dropping me off at the condo.

"I'll see you at the party," Jason said when I jumped out.

I nodded. "See you there." Then I ran upstairs.

It was so early, nobody was even awake yet. I barged into Lila's room and shook her. "Wake up!"

Lila's eyes jerked open. "What? What?"

"Did you find out what Marissa's allergic reaction to peanuts is?"

She shrugged. "No. I'm sure it's hives. What other kinds of reactions are there?"

"Lots!" I shouted. "You don't know what could happen. She could have a heart attack for all you know."

Lila rolled her eyes. "Get *out!*"

"I'm serious."

Rachel sat up in bed. "What's going on?" she asked sleepily. "What are you guys arguing about?"

"Jessica is chickening out," Lila said.

"I'm not chickening out. I'm just trying to keep you guys from making a huge mistake."

Lila narrowed her eyes. "The only person who is making a huge mistake is *you*," she said threateningly. "We have gone to a lot of trouble to make sure this surprise party gives Marissa the surprise of her life. So don't blow it. Or else."

"Does Kimberly know?"

"No," Lila said. "And if she gets wind of it, we'll know who ratted."

I went into the living room, trying to think what to do.

If I told Kimberly, it would put Kimberly in a horrible position. She'd have to put a stop to it, and that would make all the Unicorns furious with her.

If I told Marissa, she probably wouldn't even believe me. She was convinced that the Unicorns were all her close pals.

And if I told Pippa, *nobody* would ever forgive me.

I picked up the phone and dialed—hoping Jason was home already.

He was. "Listen," I said. "I need you to be my friend. I need you to do something that's going to seem very weird, but I need you to do it and not ask me why."

"OK," he agreed softly.

"I need you to come get Marissa as soon as possible and take her away for the day. Don't bring her back until late tonight."

"But . . . today is her party," Jason argued.

"Jason! I'm begging you. Just do it."

"Can't you tell me what . . ."

"No. Just please do it."

Jason let out a long sigh. "OK. I trust you. I trust you a lot. Let me see if my dad can drop me off."

I hung on for a few minutes, then he came back and told me he'd be waiting downstairs in twenty minutes.

I went into Marissa's room. Kimberly was still asleep. I put my hand over Marissa's mouth and shook her gently.

Her eyes flew open. I put my finger to my lips and gestured to her to come with me into the bathroom.

Marissa blinked and followed me. I closed the door and started whispering to her. "Jason wants to take you on a special day trip for your birthday," I said.

"Me?" she squeaked.

"Shhh!" I warned. "Don't tell anybody. Just throw on your clothes, grab your bathing suit, and go. He'll be waiting downstairs."

"But . . . but . . ."

"Don't ask questions," I warned her. "If you do, you'll ruin the surprise."

Marissa hugged me and grinned from ear to ear. "I just know this has something to do with being a Unicorn, doesn't it?"

"I can't answer any questions," I said, frowning. "But if you want to be a Unicorn, you've got to do what I tell you."

She nodded, closed her lips, and made a locking

motion. I emptied out my duffel bag and gave it to her to use.

Five minutes later we sneaked through the condo and took the elevator down. When Jason and his dad drove up, Marissa jumped into their Jeep and blew me a kiss good-bye.

I could tell that Jason was dying to ask me questions, but there was no way I could answer. So I just told them to have a great time and ran back into the building.

I was munching my cereal with a blank look on my face by the time everybody was out of bed.

"Where's Marissa?" Rachel asked sleepily, stumbling into the living room with Lila.

"She said she was going shopping," I said through a big mouthful of cereal. "She said she's looking for the perfect outfit and isn't coming home until she finds it."

Rachel and Lila looked at each other. "She knows about the party," Lila said in an exasperated voice. "Who told her?" She stared at me.

Luckily Rachel covered her face. "She must have heard me talking about it with Rafe," she groaned. "I was talking to him on the phone when she came through the room yesterday."

Lila chewed the inside of her cheek. Then she shrugged. "Doesn't matter. She thinks it's a surprise party. She just doesn't know what the surprise really is. Everything is cool."

I wonder how cool Lila's going to be when she realizes there's not going to be a birthday girl at the party.

TUESDAY, 7:00 P.M.

Dear Diary,

The guests started to arrive around three. Lila was in a total tizzy. "Where is Marissa?" she kept asking everybody.

Nobody could answer.

Rafe arrived with Larry. Both of them brought Marissa a present. Ellen took the gifts and stacked them on the coffee table. Pretty soon Carl and a bunch of girls we had met at the teen club came. They had presents too.

By three forty-five the penthouse was bulging with people, and they all wanted to know where the birthday girl was.

Lila circulated around with this frozen smile plastered on her face. "She'll be here," she kept telling everyone. "She'll be here any minute."

Rafe put on some music, and we all danced.

I danced like I have never danced before. I really let loose. I felt like it was the end of the world or something. Once the party was over, I knew I was dead meat.

By six o'clock it was pretty clear to everybody that Marissa wasn't going to show.

"Golly," Lila told people, laughing, "I guess the surprise is on us. Do we feel stupid or what? We thought of everything—except making sure that Marissa was going to be here. We kept the secret too well!"

Carl, Rafe, and Larry just laughed. "I guess Jason forgot about it too. Funny. He said he was definitely going to be here," Rafe put in.

That's when they all started to smell a rat. Every pair of Unicorn eyes turned toward me and glared. Finally the guests were gone. There was nobody to protect me. It was just me and Ellen, Mandy, Rachel, and Lila.

"I don't know what you did," Lila told me as soon as she closed the door on the last guest. "But you are going to pay for this. From now on, we are not friends. Got it? From now on, we're not even speaking to you."

I lifted my chin and reminded myself that I had done the right thing. "I don't care," I told them defiantly. (Even though I did.)

The door opened and Marissa came floating in, humming to herself. She looked like she was in a complete and total daze.

"Where have you been?" Lila demanded.

Marissa smiled—a distant, foggy smile. "Let me change, and I'll tell you all about it." Then she sort of wafted into her bedroom.

I ran out of the condo and punched the elevator button. I wanted to tell Jason what had happened. I wanted somebody to tell me what a heroine I was. How brave I was. How much better than everybody else I was.

The elevator came right away. Luckily it didn't make any stops on the way down. I ran out of the lobby and looked around for some sign of Jason.

I didn't see anything.

Then I heard someone call my name. I turned and saw Jason standing in the shadows. "I hoped you would come down," he said in a husky voice.

I ran toward him with my arms out. I knew that when I told him what I had done, he would take me in his arms and kiss me for real. Kiss me like a boyfriend.

He caught me in his arms and hugged me. "Thank you," he breathed. "Thank you for the most wonderful day of my life."

"What?"

He let go of me and held me away from him so he could look at my face. "You are incredible." He shook his head as if he were overwhelmed with admiration. "I guess you're just one of those amazingly insightful and perceptive people."

Insightful? Perceptive? *Me?*

What was he talking about?

"I'm just blown away. You knew what I didn't know. How? How did you know that Marissa and I were perfect for each other?"

An invisible fist punched me right in the stomach.

I didn't know what to do, so I just listened to Jason moon over Marissa until I couldn't stand it anymore. Finally I made some excuse and stumbled back into the building. I somehow found my way into the elevator.

Maybe this is a dream, I thought. *A nightmare.*

Maybe I would wake up and still be at the camp.

Upstairs, when I walked into the living room, Marissa was sitting there telling them all about how she and Jason had fallen madly in love and wasn't it the most wonderful birthday present in the whole world?

When she saw me, she threw herself into my arms. "Oh, Jessica. You are so sly. All this time you were just waiting for the perfect matchmaking opportunity. Fooling us all by pretending Jason was your boyfriend when you *knew* he was perfect for me."

I was so numb, so flabbergasted, and so heartbroken, I couldn't even speak.

"Well," Lila snarled when Marissa let me go. "We were so worried about you. You missed your own surprise party."

Marissa's mouth fell open. "You planned a party? For me? Oh, wow!" She opened her arms and whirled in a circle. "What a birthday! A boyfriend! A surprise party!" She gave us all a watery smile. "I'm sorry I missed it. But . . . does this mean I'm a Unicorn now?" She held up a hand. "No. No. Don't tell me. I've already had so many wonderful things happen to me today. Let's save *something* for tomorrow."

A tear trickled down her cheek. "Excuse me . . . I . . . I . . ." Her lip trembled. "I think I need to be alone for a while." She blew us all a kiss and floated back into the bedroom.

There was this long, stunned silence, then Lila threw back her head and began to laugh. "So I guess the truth about Jason is finally out."

I ran into my room. I wished like crazy that I didn't have to share it with Marissa anymore. But there was nothing I could do. I threw myself down on the bed and buried my face in my pillow to muffle my sobs.

Marissa flew over to me. "What's the matter?" she gasped. "Jessica! Talk to me."

"Nothing," I choked. "Go away."

"I'm not going away," she argued. "You're my best friend. You have to tell me what's wrong so I can make you feel better."

That did it. I sat up and just let her have it. "I am not your friend. I *hate* you!"

Marissa was so startled, she sank onto the bed.

"I hate you!" I told her again. "Get it? *Everybody* hates you, but you're just too dumb to know it."

Marissa's face turned a sickly white. "That's not true. They like me. They planned a party for me."

I shook my head. "They were planning to humiliate you. Do you know what was in that cake and in those cookies? Peanuts! They wanted you to break out in a rash in front of everybody. So I asked Jason to take you away for the day. To protect you. Ha! I should have been protecting myself. Because you stole Jason from me! And now I don't have *any* friends!"

I threw myself back down on the bed and cried some more. "I hate you, I hate you, I hate you," I said over and over into my pillow.

I don't know how long I lay there, bawling. It seemed like forever. Finally I was all out of tears. Too exhausted to cry anymore.

When I sat up and reached for a tissue, Marissa was still sitting on the end of my bed with the box in her lap. Wordlessly she handed me a tissue.

I took it and blew my nose.

We sat there for about ten minutes. Neither one of us said anything.

"Are you finished crying?" she asked finally.

I nodded.

"OK, then I have to tell you something." For once her voice sounded totally serious.

I stared at my lap, afraid to look her in the eye.

"You *are* my best friend whether you realize it or not," she told me, "because you probably saved my life."

I blew my nose again and met her gaze.

"I could have gone into a coma," she said quietly. "I might have died."

I didn't know what to say to that. I couldn't believe I had let things go as far as they had. Sure, I tried to stop it, but not hard enough.

I should have nipped the prank in the bud the minute Lila suggested it. I should have told Marissa, Kimberly, and Pippa.

I should have told the people at the camp. I should have called the police if necessary. I should have done everything humanly possible to stop it. So what if my friends got mad at me and somebody got into trouble?

You didn't risk somebody's life to keep your friends from getting into trouble!

I started to feel dizzy. To black out.

Marissa told me to lean over and hang my head between my knees. I did. Finally my chest started to relax. The dizzy feeling passed, and I could sit up. But I was hiccuping.

Marissa went into the bathroom and got me a glass of water. "Here," she said curtly. "Drink."

I took long gulps. I could feel Marissa's eyes studying me. But I couldn't look her in the face. I was too ashamed. "I am so sorry," I whispered after I finished the water.

Marissa took the glass from me. "Did Kimberly know about this?" she asked.

Now I did look at her. I looked her in the eye because she had to know that I was telling the truth. "No. They made sure Kimberly didn't know."

Marissa's face was pale. "*That's* a relief. I thought maybe my own cousin was trying to murder me."

Murder!

I started shaking. I couldn't stop. I just shook and shook. Marissa put her arms around me. "It's OK," she told me. "It's OK."

"No, it's not," I sobbed. "It's not OK. Nothing is OK. We're not having fun. Everybody including me is being horrible. And we almost killed you. How can you say everything is OK?"

She gave me a crooked smile. "I don't know. In spite of everything, I feel great. I'm in love with Jason, and he's in love with me. OK. Maybe it's not *love*, but it's a mutual crush. My first! And this summer has been great for me up until now. You just don't understand what it's been like for me. Nobody knows what the real story is."

I sat back and leaned against the pillows. "What is the real story?"

"This food allergy thing has taken over my

whole life. I've had to be so careful. And my mother is so conditioned to be overprotective, she doesn't know when to turn it off. She's never let me go to regular school. This year will be my first year to go to school with other kids."

"You're kidding!"

"No. I always had home tutors. But I told my mom I really wanted to go to regular school next year. That I had to. That I was just dying of loneliness. She said absolutely not, and we had this huge fight about it. I wound up running away, and the police brought me back home. That's why I'm spending the summer with Pippa. Mom and I agreed we needed some time apart. And it was a good way for me to prove I could make friends and take responsibility for my diet."

"I had no idea," I whispered.

Marissa looked shamefaced. "I didn't want you guys to know. Kimberly knew, but she promised not to tell anybody."

I looked at Marissa and suddenly saw her the way Rafe and Jason and Peter saw her. I saw someone with a lot of courage and spirit. Somebody who always had a smile for everyone. Somebody who wasn't too cool to care.

"So what do you want to do about this peanut ambush thing?" I asked her.

She bit her lip. "I want to sleep on it."

Fifteen

◇

Dear Diary,

It's a gorgeous day, but I don't think I'll ever feel happy again. I woke up this morning with a horrible headache from crying. My guts were in a total uproar over all the ugly stuff that had been said. And my heart was breaking.

Marissa got up early to meet Jason for a swim and a walk on the beach.

I stayed in the room. I was too humiliated, angry, and disgusted to face the others.

After a little while Kimberly came in. Pippa had picked her up, and they were both home. She was holding a note that Rachel had left on the refrigerator. The note said everybody had gone snorkeling at Malaka Cove again.

"How come you didn't go?" Kimberly asked me.

I shrugged and doodled in the margin of my diary.

"You guys all had a big fight, didn't you?" She rolled her eyes upward. "Is that why your eyes are all red?"

"Yeah," I admitted. "We did have a fight. The usual stuff. Lila trying to make me miserable and succeeding." I didn't tell Kimberly about the surprise party. She would have gone through the roof.

Kimberly flopped back on the bed and stared at the ceiling. "I'm glad this stuff is over for me," she said finally.

That surprised me. "What do you mean?" I asked.

She sat up and ran her hand through her hair. Kimberly suddenly looked a lot older than the rest of us. I can't explain it, but she seemed to have grown up over the past few weeks. "Don't get me wrong. I'm glad everybody could come on this trip. But I'm losing interest in being part of a group. I think I'd rather be myself."

I drew in my breath. "That's exactly what I've been thinking."

"I'm going to high school!" Kimberly exclaimed. "Why am I worrying about what Lila or Janet Howell or Peter Feldman thinks? I don't even like them. What's the point of getting older if you're not going to grow up?" She grinned. "Guess what I realized over the weekend?"

"What?"

"I'm really pretty. And guys like me."

I smiled. "Oh, yeah? Like who?"

Kimberly batted her eyelashes. "Steve. I hope you guys don't mind, but I'm probably not going back with you. I'm going to stay on until the day before school. I already asked Pippa. That way I can spend some quality time with Steve."

I knew where Kimberly was coming from. She was feeling confident, so she didn't need our approval. She was pulling away from the Unicorns.

If she could do it, I could do it. I took a deep breath and sat up. "There's something I haven't told you."

"What?"

I gave Kimberly the rundown on how the Unicorns planned a surprise party and laced everything with peanuts.

Kimberly's face turned purple. I swear. I have never seen anybody look so angry in my whole life.

"That does it," she fumed, standing up and pacing. "They're out of here. All of them. That's the most irresponsible, cold-blooded, evil thing I have ever heard in my life. I'm going to tell Pippa and—"

"Wait! I have a better idea. I tried to tell Lila that food allergies could be dangerous. She wouldn't listen. Some people you can't tell. Some people you have to show."

I told her what I had in mind.

She began to laugh.

"Think Marissa will go for it?" I asked.

Kimberly nodded. "In a big way. She's your number-one fan, Jessica. I think she'll do whatever you think is right."

I couldn't help feeling proud. I've never had

what you would call—"leadership quality." But knowing somebody looked up to me made me want to stand tall.

THURSDAY, *11:40* A.M.

Dear Diary,

Tonight's the night. Marissa's birthday dinner! We're going to a fancy luau.

Let the games begin.

THURSDAY, *10:00* P.M.

Dear Diary,

Tonight was actually a lot of fun. We were all dressed up, and Pippa hired a stretch limo to take us to the restaurant—a gorgeous place high up on a mountainside.

Under the circumstances, it was impossible to keep up the grudge match. So by the time we hit the restaurant, we were all laughing and talking just like nothing had ever happened.

Pippa told us we could invite whoever we wanted. So Kimberly asked Steve. Marissa asked Jason. I asked Carl.

And Ellen and Rachel asked Rafe and Larry. *But they still didn't know who was with who!* It was pretty funny when we tried to sit down. There was a lot of hesitating/lurching/sitting/standing-back-up-and-saying-"oops" stuff.

Larry finally wound up sitting at one end of the table—next to Pippa. And Rafe wound up sitting at the other end—next to Jason.

Aside from Pippa, the only two people who didn't have dates were Mandy and Lila. Lila kept checking to make sure her mobile phone was on "in case Wiley called." (I guess she thought the phone counted as a date.)

If I hadn't known what was coming, I would have teased her about it. But I knew she was going to get a big shock later. (Turns out she got an even bigger shock than I planned—but I'll get to that.)

Dinner was *fantastic*. Afterward we danced on this big black-and-white forties-style dance floor. While Carl and I were dancing, I noticed that his eyes kept wandering back to the table. He was looking at Mandy.

Mandy sat at the table, staring down at her lap. I realized that she was miserable. Not about Carl. But about the whole situation. Mandy wasn't naturally cruel, but she'd somehow let herself fall under Lila's evil spell.

I decided to see if I could break that spell. When Carl excused himself to go talk to the DJ, I went over to the table. Lila, who was still making a point of not speaking to me, left and went to the ladies' room.

"Mandy," I said, "I probably shouldn't be sticking my nose into anybody else's business, but I think Carl is interested in you."

Mandy's eyes lit up, and her face looked happy for the first time in days. "Really? But . . . I thought he liked you."

"He does. As a friend. But I think he may have a crush on you. You like him, don't you?"

Mandy bit her lip, hesitating. I guess she wasn't

sure whether she should confide in me or not.

"If you do, you've got to act different. Every time he tries to talk to you, you act like he's invisible."

Mandy blushed. "I'm trying to be cool."

"Don't," I told her bluntly. "Smile. Ask him about surfing. Quit acting like you couldn't care less if he lives or dies. Here he comes." I waved him over.

"Jessica! No!" Mandy hissed.

Carl came toward the table, smiling uncertainly. "Mandy wants to dance," I said with all the tact and subtlety of, say, Marissa.

"Jessica!" Mandy practically shrieked.

Carl's eyebrows flew up. "With me?"

"Sure, with you," I answered.

He looked at her. "Do you?" he asked uneasily, as if he half expected her to angrily refuse.

Mandy's face was bright red, but she couldn't help smiling. "OK," she said.

I kicked her under the table.

"I'd love to," she corrected herself.

Pretty soon she and Carl were boogying away. Lila came back to the table and sat way on the other side so she wouldn't have to talk to me.

I smiled behind my hand. Pippa had gone to another table to visit with some friends, but now she was on her way back. Her friends were leaving the restaurant. We were the last table of people left.

It was time for the floor show.

The music came to an end, and Pippa signaled everybody to come back to the table. When they had taken their places, she tapped her water glass and stood. "A toast. To Marissa on her birthday."

Everybody lifted their water glasses and clinked them together.

Kimberly stood up. "I just want to say a few words about Marissa and how special she's made this house party."

Marissa smiled and gave Jason a pleased nudge with her shoulder.

"I know that everybody feels the same way," Kimberly continued, addressing her remarks to Marissa. "They tried to show you before by giving you a surprise party. But you missed it. Fortunately I found the cake, and I saved a piece of it for you." Kimberly opened a silver box that she had brought from Pippa's new gift shop. She took out a small plate with several broken pieces of cake on it.

I looked around the table. Every Unicorn face was frozen.

"I say let's all take a bite for luck and to seal our friendship. Marissa, the first bite goes to you."

Mandy half stood. "Wait!" she yelled.

But it was too late. Marissa had snatched a piece of the cake from the plate in Kimberly's hand and popped it into her mouth. She chewed with a big smile.

Two seconds later her eyes bugged. Her hand flew to her throat. She staggered out of her chair.

"Marissa!" Pippa shouted, lurching toward her. "What is it? What's the matter?" She sounded so concerned that for a moment I forgot she was in on the whole thing.

Marissa made some horrible choking, gagging noises and fell down on the floor. Her eyelids fluttered, then closed.

Jason knelt beside her. He felt her wrist. He felt her neck. He leaned over and listened to her heart. His face registered shock. "She's dead," he croaked. "She's *dead!*" He lifted Marissa's limp figure and buried his face in her shoulder. "Marissa!" he sobbed. "Marissa, come back!"

No one said a word. No one moved. Then Ellen's hands flew to her face. Mandy's knees wobbled, and she collapsed into her chair. Rachel burst into hysterical tears.

I stood up and pointed at Lila. "Murderer!" I accused.

"No!" Lila shrieked. She was positively green.

"You killed her," I said through gritted teeth. "I told you she was allergic to peanuts. But you wouldn't listen."

Pippa glared at Lila. "You did this on purpose?" she raged. "On *purpose?* You're a killer!"

"We all did it," Mandy wailed, pulling at her braids. "We're all guilty. Oh, my God! How could we do this? How?"

"That's what I want to know!" Marissa said angrily, miraculously coming back from the dead.

Every single Unicorn screamed. Ellen and Rachel thumped right into Carl and Rafe. They fell over their chairs and tumbled to the floor.

On the way down Rafe tried to grab the edge of the table and got the tablecloth instead.

Crash!

The whole cloth came sliding off the table, complete with dessert plates, water glasses, and what sounded like a thousand knives and forks.

Larry tried to keep the big silver water bucket from falling over but wound up spilling it. Icy water poured right into Lila's lap. She let out a scream that could have awakened the dead but instead startled Mandy, who fell backward in her chair so that she lay on the floor with her feet pointing straight up in the air.

It was pandemonium!

I started laughing so hard, I fell out of my own seat.

Marissa and Jason were both hysterical with laughter, and Pippa was pounding the table.

Just then the phone rang. The phone in Lila's purse. She snatched it out of her bag. "Hello?" she said in a faint voice.

It was Wiley.

And guess what?

He was calling to break up!

Could life get any better than this?

No way.

And so, Dear Diary, by the time we all got back to the condo, everybody had apologized to everybody. Everybody agreed that Marissa was an incredible actress. Everybody agreed that it was a night they would never forget.

And everybody agreed that since we only had two days left—we should devote ourselves to having fun and stop torturing each other.

Can we actually do it?

I'll find out starting tomorrow.

Sixteen

Dear Diary,

I'm sitting on the beach. I only have two more pages left in this notebook and today is our last day, so I guess I'll come out even.

We did have a good last few days. We had a lot of parties and group outings. But talk about ironic! Lila and I were the only two Unicorns who didn't have a guy of our own.

In fact, we're the only two Unicorns sitting on the beach right now watching the sun go down. Everybody else is saying a romantic good-bye to someone special.

I guess Rachel, Ellen, Rafe, and Larry finally got things figured out. Because I saw Rachel and Larry walk off in one direction and Ellen and Rafe walk off in another.

Lila cried for a whole day about Wiley. But she'd

learned her lesson. We didn't see any more Janet Howell behavior. She was also good and ashamed of herself over what she tried to do to Marissa.

School starts in a week.

I hope we don't all get split up. But if we do, I know now that it'll be OK. I'll make new friends if I have to. I sure learned how to do that this summer.

And if I have to let some old friendships go, well, I can do that too. I still love Lila. But I'm not sure I like her, if you know what I mean. I'm not sure she likes me either.

But I guess if I learned anything at all, it's this: I'd rather like myself than be liked.

No more room left.

Just the margin.

Aloha!

Good-bye and hello!

Will Jessica have to say good-bye to the Unicorns? Find out in the brand-new series, Sweet Valley Jr. High!

Bantam Books in the SWEET VALLEY TWINS series.
Ask your bookseller for the books you have missed.

This fall, don't let the summer end!

Find out how your favorite twins spent their summer in these two special-edition diaries!

ISBN: 0-553-49237-3

ISBN: 0-553-48607-1

Elizabeth came to Costa Rica for the summer to work hard and help people. Instead, it's a nonstop party. Not that she's complaining. But what has she gotten herself into?

Jessica went to Hawaii with her friends and _no_ parents. Sounds like the combination for the ultimate summer vacation. Instead it's freaky—her friends don't seem the same and she can't tell if it's they who have changed or her. . . .

ON SALE OCTOBER AND NOVEMBER 1998!

And don't miss a totally **new Sweet Valley**—New Attitude, New Look, New Everything.

Bantam
Bantam Doubleday Dell

Sweet Valley Jr. High coming in January 1999!

BFYR 187